Out of the Ashes
by
Olivia Duncan Craig

Contact the Author:
www.oliviaduncancraig.com
oliviaduncancraig@gmail.com

*O*nce upon a time, in the region of Virginia known as Horse Country, there lived a boy named Noah. He was beautiful and good, and his parents, who had tried for many years to have children before being blessed with their son, loved him more than anything in the world.

"My sweet angel," his mother whispered to him one night, soon after he was born. "Sleep easy. Know your father and I love you, and will look out for you. As long as we're alive, you'll never have to worry. You'll always be our first concern."

Little Noah was far too young to understand her words. But he could feel her warmth and the caring in her touch, so he slept, secure in her arms and with his place in the world.

Sadly, such security was not to last. His mother, lovely yet never strong, fell ill not long after Noah had taken his first steps. She failed to recover and was gone before Noah had celebrated his second birthday.

With her death, Noah's father was all but inconsolable. Neither he nor his wife had any brothers or sisters, and her parents were dead. All that was left to him was his baby boy and his own mother, who lived in a faraway place called Florida. Because she loved her son and grandson, Noah's grandmother left her home by the ocean and traveled many miles to be with her family in their time of need.

"My darling boy," she told Noah's father, looking deep into his eyes. "I know you loved your wife, as I did, and that you'll never stop missing her. But you need to be strong for Noah's sake. He's so little, and only has you to depend on now."

"Noah means the world to me," Noah's father said. "But I have responsibilities outside our home. I can't be with him every hour of the day. I worry he'll be lonely and not have the attention he needs."

"Then you'll have to marry again," the grandmother said.

"Mother, I can't," Noah's father replied, shaking his head. "I'm not ready. I may never be ready."

The grandmother took his hands and smiled, though her eyes were very grave. "You're right in saying your son will need companionship, a mother who can be there to wipe away his tears and other children to play with and learn from. I'll help in every way I can. But I'm an old woman, and may not live to see Noah become an adult."

Noah's father smiled at his mother, and squeezed her narrow hands gently in his grasp. "I can't ask you to leave your life behind for us."

"Don't be ridiculous," said the grandmother. "You're not asking. I'm offering it freely, because I love my grandchild and you, and want to be here to watch Noah grow. I'll stay until you're married again."

Convinced by his mother's persuasive tongue, Noah's father allowed himself ample time to mourn, then set about finding a new wife. He had no shortage of women to pursue. His hair may have begun to turn silver, but he remained fit and trim, smiled easily, and acted in no way other than with kindness.

More importantly in the eyes of many prospective brides, he was as wealthy as any in the land. He had spent many years in The District as a man of great power and influence before leaving for the hills of Virginia to start a family and pursue his true passion, raising horses. His coffers were full, and his reputation was that of a generous man.

In the months that followed, he dated dozens of women, searching for one who was attractive, intelligent and potentially a good mother for Noah. It took him more than a year. But when he met Elaine, he believed he'd found the perfect woman to help him raise his son.

Elaine was younger than him by several years, beautiful, and had grown up in the land of Texas. She came from humble beginnings and had worked hard to build a life for herself. She was well-educated, well-traveled, and shared his love of horses. Most importantly, like Noah's father, she'd recently lost her first love, and been left alone with children. Two in Elaine's case—a daughter named Lucy who was two years younger than Noah and a son named Dillon who was three years older.

Noah's father watched Elaine with her children and with Noah when she would visit. He was pleased by what he saw. Her own children seemed to adore her, and she was patient and kind with Noah. While what he felt for Elaine was far from passion, she was someone with whom he could see spending the rest of his life.

"It's finally happened, Mother. I've found the one," Noah's father told his mother. "I've asked Elaine to be my bride and she's accepted. We're going to be married as soon as possible."

"Are you sure?" Noah's grandmother asked. She had been the one to urge him in this direction; that was true. Yet all the same, she was concerned. Noah's mother had been everything she could have wished for in a daughter-in-law—gentle and giving, warm and good. And what was more, her son had truly loved his wife. She wanted the same for him with his new bride.

Noah's father smiled. "I'm as sure as I can be. Don't worry. Please. Just be happy for us. For Noah and me, both."

"Of course, sweetheart," she assured him, stretching up to press a kiss to his cheek. "I'm as happy as can be. Go and tell your boy."

Noah's father went in search of his son, finding him in his playroom, surrounded by his things—stuffed animals and games, books and puzzles. Noah's father knew he was guilty of indulging his son. Yet Noah was such a good little boy, he didn't see the harm in spoiling him just a bit.

"Daddy!" Noah cried when he saw him, scrambling up from where he sat, playing with his blocks, and rushing on sturdy legs to his father's side.

Noah's father laughed as he scooped up his son and held him high in his arms like an airplane.

"Have you missed me, Noey?" Noah's father asked, drawing him near.

"All the time," Noah said, winding his arms tight around his father's neck.

Noah's father chuckled and settled them both in the corner rocking chair, Noah perched sideways on his lap. He looked just like his mother, his son did, with his dark brown hair and equally dark eyes. "I need to ask you something very important, Noah. Can you listen close and give me an honest answer?"

Noah looked up at his father, attentive and subdued. "Yes,

Daddy."

"Good boy," Noah's father said, smiling down at him. "Tell me, what do you think of Elaine?"

Noah thought hard, his brow wrinkling with effort. "She's pretty."

"Yes, she is. What else?"

"She talks funny."

"She's from Texas. People from there have a kind of...drawl. I think it's nice, once you get used to it."

"I guess."

"What about Lucy and Dillon? Do you like them?"

Noah looked down at his fingers and shrugged. He was playing with his father's tie. "They're okay. Lucy is just a baby and Dillon won't play with me."

"Well, Dillon is older than you," his father said, rescuing his tie. "Once you grow up some, he might be more willing."

Noah nodded, but said nothing further.

Noah's father hesitated before he spoke again. "What would you think about them living here—Elaine and Lucy and Dillon? Would you like that, to have a mommy and a brother and sister?"

Noah raised his head and looked up at his father, concern shining in his eyes. "Where will you be?"

"Here, of course," his father said, surprised. "With you."

Noah searched his father's face before the corners of his mouth lifted, tentative and slow. The boy had dimples. His father loved to see him smile. "Good."

"So that would be all right then—if Elaine came with her children to live with us? If we all became a family?"

"If you want."

Noah's father hugged him to his chest. The little boy sighed and cuddled close, his hands clenched tight in his father's shirt, holding on.

They were going to be part of a family again, Noah's father thought as he rocked Noah, snug in his arms.

He was going to give his son the life he deserved.

~*~*~*~

Noah's father married Elaine in June, just a month before Noah's fifth birthday. The wedding was held at Noah's home. People came from as far away as California to attend. Noah was his father's best man.

Noah had never been to a wedding before and was nervous with all the people and the crowds and the noise. He knew his father was excited and wanted him to be excited too. And Noah tried, really he did. But part of him was scared. He liked living in his home with Daddy and Grandma, with a room filled with toys that were his alone, and quiet Saturday mornings with Grandma in the kitchen cooking pancakes, while Daddy and he watched cartoons in their pajamas. He liked how things had always been. Now they would be different.

And no matter what his father told him, Noah wasn't entirely convinced different could be better.

But this was what his father wanted, and more than anything Noah wanted him to be happy. So he stood tall in front of the minister as his father watched Elaine walk down the aisle, her long blonde hair swept up and away beneath her veil like a queen wearing a crown. Noah smiled up at his father, not fidgeting a bit, and didn't even lose the ring he'd been told to hold on to. And if he was worried when Elaine later kissed Dillon and Lucy but not him, or when his father talked about perhaps keeping all the children's toys stored in Noah's playroom, he tried hard not to show it. He was polite and quiet, and a very good boy.

Just like always.

When his birthday came in July, Noah wondered if perhaps his father had noticed his efforts, because he told Noah he had an extra special surprise waiting for him outside.

"Come with me out to the paddock, Noah," his father said to him the morning Noah turned five. "I want to show you something."

Noah followed, eager and curious. His father didn't like Noah near the horses unless they were together. He always told Noah the animals were too big and too easily startled for a little boy to play near them all by himself. It was a bright, sunny morning, warm, but without the terrible humidity that made some Virginia days so uncomfortable in summer.

When they got to the part of the property where the horses were kept, Noah's father motioned to Jack, their stable hand. With a nod, Jack went inside the barn.

"What do you want me to see, Daddy?" Noah asked, climbing up on the fence, his feet balanced on the lowest rung, his hands curved, clinging, around the top.

"Your birthday present," his father said, lifting him up so he could sit on the highest rail.

Moments later, Jack led out a spindly-legged colt, who looked as if he couldn't be more than a few days old. He was black with white socks and a splotch of white in the center of his forehead.

Noah gasped and nearly fell from his place on the fence. He'd only ever been riding with his father on a palomino named Sundance. Noah would sit in the saddle in front of his father and the two of them would trot around the ring and sometimes walk the property.

But this...

Did his father mean this might actually be his?

Jack walked the colt up to Noah and his father. Noah reached out a trembling hand to pet the youngster, as softly and gently as he could. He slid his palm down from the little fellow's forehead to his nose. His muzzle felt like velvet, and he had lashes longer than any Noah had ever seen.

"Do you like him?" Noah's father asked.

"Yes," Noah whispered, afraid to jump to any conclusions. Maybe his father had only brought him out there to see the colt, maybe he didn't intend to actually give him to Noah.

Yet Noah hoped. He really, really hoped...

"He's too little to ride now," his father said, stretching out his hand to pat the colt on his neck. "He needs to grow up some, like you. But I thought you might like to meet him now, so you can spend time with him as he grows, get to know him as he gets to know you. That way, when he's ready to be ridden, you'll already be friends. Happy birthday, Noah."

Noah had no words, except, "Daddy!"

Without fear of falling or injury, he launched himself into his father's arms, hugging him with all his might. "Thank you, thank you. Thank you so much!"

His father laughed, and swept Noah up against his chest, hugging him back. "You're very welcome."

"I'll take such good care of him. You'll see! I'll feed him, and...and play with him. And I'll come out to visit him every day. I'll make sure he's never lonely."

"I know you will. I know. Do you have any idea what you want to name him?"

"I get to name him?"

"Absolutely. He's your horse."

Noah pulled back from his father's embrace and looked over the fence at the colt. The little horse met his gaze calmly, his large liquid eyes seeming to Noah to be not only friendly, but wise. Noah bit his lower lip and thought hard. Naming something—someone—was a very big responsibility. He wanted to be certain and get it right.

And suddenly a name popped into Noah's head, one he wondered if the colt had magically placed there himself.

"Midnight," he told his father.

"Midnight?" his father echoed back with a smile. "You've never stayed up that late in your life. What made you choose that?"

Noah looked at the colt again, trying to decide what had truly made the name come to mind. "Well...he's dark like nighttime. And the white on his face there kind of looks like a star."

Noah's father leaned closer to the colt as if inspecting the mark. "Why so it does. Seems to me as if you've made an excellent choice. Midnight, it is."

In answer, the little horse whinnied, almost as if he understood.

"I think he approves!" Noah's father said, grinning.

Noah grinned back at him, his smile so broad his cheeks began to hurt. This was the best birthday ever. He didn't think he could ever remember being happier.

That feeling stayed with him the entire day, through his grandmother's pancake breakfast, through the backyard party in the afternoon, and the evening spent opening up presents and eating way too much birthday cake and ice cream.

When his father carried him up to bed that night, Noah's head heavy on his father's shoulder, Noah thought about how lucky he was. About his life, and his new family—Elaine, who still looked at him as if he were a mystery, baby Lucy, and Dillon, who was away at camp.

He didn't really know them yet, any more than he knew Midnight. But he had time. As long as his father was there to guide him, to guide them all, everything would be all right. Noah was sure they could become the family his father hoped they would become.

The day after Noah's birthday, morning dawned bright and warm and full of promise. Noah slept unaware, still exhausted from too much excitement and too many sweets. But his father was up early, his schedule packed with appointments and errands that couldn't wait for a less hectic day.

Before he left, he went into Noah's room to say goodbye. Yet when he saw his son was still asleep, he didn't wake him. Instead, he ran his hand over Noah's rumpled hair, brushing it away from Noah's face. Bending down, he pressed a kiss to his son's smooth brow.

"Have a good day, little man," Noah's father whispered. Noah stirred, but didn't waken. His father smiled and pulled the covers up over Noah's shoulders, his hand lingering there for just a moment before leaving Noah to his rest. "I love you."

The day passed quickly. One destination led to another for Noah's father, with little to connect them but the highway in between.

He ate lunch at a roadside diner, called Steak and Eggs, bargaining between bites with another man over the price of a stallion he was considering adding to his stable. While Noah's father walked away from their conversation feeling optimistic, all the talk of bloodlines and stud fees had given him indigestion.

I'm getting old, he thought, paying the bill. My stomach can't handle a double cheeseburger and fries unless it's followed by antacids for dessert. What he really looked forward to these days was dinner with his new family. Elaine was an excellent cook.

By the time he was on his way home, rush hour had begun. The highway was crowded with commuters and interstate truckers, yet traffic moved along at a respectable pace. Noah's father was pleased. With a little luck, he'd have time to play with Noah before Elaine called everyone in for the evening meal.

On a particularly winding stretch of road, he got boxed in behind a massive moving van, hauling some household's possessions to destinations unknown. Despite its engines working hard, the truck was traveling far slower than Noah's father would have liked. He saw an opening in traffic, and was just about to pull out from in back of the semi, when one of its tires exploded. The pieces flew like shrapnel and struck the windshield of his car.

He dodged without thinking, setting off a chain reaction across all lanes. Horns blared and tires squealed. Before he fully realized what was happening, Noah's father lost control. He swerved, his car hitting the guardrail on an overpass, then tumbling over to land on the road below. He was killed upon impact.

Word got back to the family hours later. Noah was already in his pajamas when the phone call came, announcing the awful news.

When Noah's grandmother learned of her son's death, she took to her bed. On the day he was laid to rest, she collapsed at the gravesite. The doctors later said she'd suffered a stroke. They were unsure if she would ever fully recover.

In a matter of days, Noah's world came crashing down around him.

What the poor boy didn't know was things were going to get far worse before they got better.

~*~*~*~

While young Noah was learning about love and loss, another little boy was living a decidedly more charmed life.

His name was Matthew and he lived halfway between Dallas and Wichita in a region known as North Texas Horse Country. He was four years older than Noah.

If Noah's father maintained a healthy bank account, Matthew's father was Texas royalty. The family fortune had been made generations before through railroads, oil and cattle, and as years had passed, the holdings had grown ever more diversified and vast. Matthew's father ruled an empire, and he hoped one day Matthew, his only child, would willingly inherit his throne.

"I'm going to give him the world," Matthew's father had told his wife when Matthew was still in his bassinet.

"Just make sure you give him plenty of love first," Matthew's mother had replied, as wise as she was good.

Matthew's father had smiled, kissed her cheek, and agreed to do just that.

So while Matthew grew up with every advantage—a beautiful home with its own swimming pool, stable and tennis courts; tutors in piano, horseback riding and golf; travel to places like Europe, Asia and Australia; and virtually any toy or gadget that caught his eye—he was also taught the importance of responsibility and respect. He learned that just because his family had money, he was no better than anyone else. He had chores to do and grades to maintain, and if he failed with either, there were consequences. His parents raised him to be good and kind and brave. And most importantly, they loved him as much as two parents had ever loved a child. Recognizing how fortunate he was, Matthew loved them back and tried very hard to please them. He was a happy child who wanted others to feel as he did.

"Sometimes your family gives me the creeps," said Cal, who was Matthew's friend and the son of the man who looked after Matthew's family's estate.

"Why would you say something like that?" Matthew asked.

It was the summer before Matthew started fourth grade. He

was nine years old. Cal was four years older, with sun bleached hair and more freckles than Matthew. Their age difference didn't seem to matter, though. Cal visited his father at work all the time, and had let Matthew tag along after him ever since Matthew could walk. That morning, they'd saddled two of Matthew's father's award-winning quarter horses and ridden out until the hot Texas sun had become too much to bear. Having come back to the house for lunch, they were letting their food settle beneath Matthew's favorite oak tree, before putting on their trunks and spending the afternoon by the pool.

"Because it's true," Cal said, leaning back against the tree's rough and tender bark. "You're perfect. All of you. It ain't natural."

Matthew scowled. "We aren't perfect. Why would you say something like that?"

Cal rolled his eyes. "Are you kidding me? Your daddy is rich, your momma is pretty, you're a straight A student and everybody's friend. You all get along and are nice to other people, no matter how much money they have. You're like some kind of robo-family at Disney World. I'm telling you—it's creepy."

Shaking his head, Matthew picked up a small branch and began scratching his name in the dirt near his hip, cursive-style, taking care to keep from breaking the line. "Would it make you feel better if I was really mean to you? Called you names or told lies about you or hit you or something? Would that make it feel less creepy?"

Cal looked over at him and smiled. "Would you do that if I asked you to?"

Matthew met Cal's eyes and frowned even harder. Cal's smile widened.

Sometimes Matthew didn't understand Cal even a little bit. He teased Matthew all the time, yet defended him like a lion would its cub if anyone else tried to do the same. He called Matthew names like 'kid' and 'son,' but always made a point of including him, even when Cal's friends urged him to leave 'the baby' behind. He was Matthew's best friend, so Matthew wanted to say the right thing, but he had no idea what that might be.

"I guess so," Matthew said at last, taking a chance it was what Cal wanted to hear. "I could probably be mean sometimes if that would make you happy."

Cal's smile turned into a laugh. He reached out and shoved Matthew's shoulder, rocking Matthew where he sat. "Son, let me give you some words of advice. When the time comes, make sure you marry someone as nice as you."

Matthew was nine years old. He wasn't exactly thinking about marriage just yet. "What are you talking about?" he asked, tossing away his stick.

Cal continued as if he hadn't heard Matthew's question. "You're way too nice for your own good. If you're not careful, some pretty face is going to walk all over you."

Matthew blushed, then looked away. He hated when his cheeks turned pink almost as much as he hated his freckles. "I'm not that nice."

"Don't be ashamed of it," Cal advised him. "Just make sure the people you're being nice to deserve it. Like I've told you before—it's no sin to give an ass-kicking to someone who's got one coming."

Now it was Matthew's turn to laugh. "You hear that in church last week or something?"

Cal grinned. "The Gospel According to Cal. Stick with me, kid. I'll make a believer out of you yet."

What was left of Noah's summer after his father had died and his grandmother fell ill wasn't spent riding, or swimming, or lazing beneath a spreading oak with his best friend. Instead, he spent most of it tucked away inside. People poured into and out of the house daily in waves. He would hear the voices downstairs, the opening and closing of doors, and bodies moving about. But few of the guests ever came upstairs to visit, and he was only ever allowed to come down—or go outside to visit Midnight—when their visitors had gone for the day.

With Dillon still away at camp, Elaine had hired a nanny to look after Lucy and Noah while she did whatever it was she was doing. Noah didn't know what that might be. He didn't see Elaine much either.

The nanny was young and smiled often. Her name was Sarah. She had wavy brown hair down to her shoulders and a tiny mole near the corner of her mouth. She talked to Noah with a quiet voice and touched him often with gentle hands. Noah knew she wanted to cheer him up. She tried to include him in games she would play with Lucy, and urged him to watch television with them. But Noah didn't respond. He couldn't.

It was as if part of him had died when his father had, or at least had gotten lost. Nothing made sense to him anymore. He couldn't think, couldn't understand. It was all so confusing. How could his father have been there one minute, then gone the next? And why wouldn't anyone let him see his grandmother?

He asked about her all the time.

"When is Grandma coming home?" he would say to Sarah.

Yet even though it seemed she was always encouraging him to speak, whenever Noah asked this particular question, Sarah would look uncomfortable and have trouble meeting his eyes. "She's very sick, Noah. She needs to stay in the hospital awhile longer."

"Can I see her?"

"Not just yet."

"When then?"

"Why don't you ask your mother?"

That was the truly strange thing. Noah no longer had the father he adored. But now he had a mother he barely knew. Well...a stepmother anyway. She was the one he had to depend on for everything, the one he had to ask permission from. Yet it seemed to Noah as if his stepmother were avoiding him, and he couldn't figure out why.

Noah spent most days in the playroom with Lucy. Sarah even brought their meals to them there. Yet, when it was time for bed, it was Sarah who made sure Noah washed his face and brushed his teeth, Sarah who tucked him in, even though Noah would hear Elaine come upstairs to say goodnight to Lucy. He couldn't understand why she didn't visit his room too. She was as much his momma now as Lucy's, wasn't she? Didn't his daddy say they were all going to be a family together?

Then early one morning, Noah woke to an especially loud commotion on the first floor. Before he could investigate the cause, he heard Elaine's footsteps on the stairs. He was surprised when rather than walking past his room as she had so often before, she opened the door and looked in at him with what Noah thought might be disapproval.

"Noah, you lazy boy. You need to get dressed and come downstairs. The movers are here and want to begin packing on this floor. You need to be out of the way."

"Packing?" Noah said, still half asleep. "Where are we going?"

"No place you need to concern yourself with," she said, her expression calm, yet somehow foreboding. "Get up and get dressed. Sarah will take Lucy and you outside for the day."

"Yes, Ma'am," Noah said, slipping out from beneath the covers, rubbing his eyes with his fists to try and wake up.

"Oh, Noah. One more thing."

Standing beside his bed, Noah peered up at Elaine. She looked as she always did, beautiful, like something out of a picture book, her blonde hair hanging sleek and long, framing a face with features as even and perfect as a mask. Noah had no idea what she was thinking. It worried him that he never did. "Before you go downstairs, go into the playroom and choose a toy to take with you," she said.

"To take with me?" Noah echoed with a frown. "Take with me where? Outside? Why only one? What about my other toys?"

"The rest will boxed up and given to charity," Elaine said. "Dillon is too old to play with most of them and Lucy really prefers her dolls. I'm not taking all that paraphernalia with us when we move."

"But what about me?" Noah asked, taking a step towards her. "They're my toys. Why are you giving them away?"

"Because you're a spoiled little boy who has more toys than any one child needs," Elaine said, her voice hardening. "Your father indulged you far too much. I won't be making that same mistake."

"That's not fair—"

"If you argue any further, Noah, you'll have no toys at all," Elaine said, folding her arms. "Now I suggest you get dressed and do as I say. Don't forget, I'm your mother now. It wouldn't do to provoke me."

Trembling with a mix of indignation and fear, Noah swallowed back all the things he wanted to say, and nodded.

"Good. I'll see you downstairs."

Noah hurriedly pulled on clothes, wearing the same jeans as the day before and a different T-shirt. From downstairs, he could hear male voices he didn't recognize, calling to one another from the open front door.

"How many boxes do you think we're gonna need?"

"Don't know. I haven't been upstairs yet. Bring in that first bunch and we'll see how many more after that."

Worried the movers would get to his toys before he'd had the chance to make his selection, Noah hurried down the hallway and ducked into the playroom. Closing the door behind him, he leaned his back against it and looked around him, overwhelmed by the task at hand.

How could he ever make a choice?

Should he take his Legos? His fire truck? One of his puzzles or maybe a favorite book?

Noah stood there, frozen in indecision, with too much to think about and not nearly enough time.

Then he heard footsteps on the stairs. He didn't want to be there when the movers—or worse, Elaine—made it to the second floor.

All at once, he knew what he couldn't live without.

He reached past all the shiny cars and trucks, the colorful board games and scary plastic dinosaurs, to pull from the shelf a faded stuffed animal. He was a white dog with black spots, floppy black ears and dark button eyes. His name was Tommy. He'd been in Noah's life for as long as Noah could remember. His father had told him once his mother had brought Tommy home from the store before Noah had even been born.

"He's going to want a dog, you know," his father had told Noah his mother had said. "All little boys do. This can be his first. A placeholder until he's old enough for the real thing."

Noah used to sleep with Tommy when he was very little. He'd liked the way the dog's small soft body had fit in the crook of his arm. But as he had grown older, he'd needed his stuffed friend less and less, and Tommy's place had gone from Noah's pillow to the toy shelf. Now though, with everything that was happening in Noah's life, he thought it might be nice to keep a friendly face close by. Even one with button eyes.

"Come on, Tommy," Noah murmured, clutching the little dog to his chest. "Let's get out of here."

Together, they made their way towards the stairs. Noah just wished he knew a way the two of them could not only escape from the playroom, but go back in time.

Not a week later, Noah was climbing into the backseat of the family car. Lucy scrambled up to sit beside him. Sarah was behind the wheel. They were preparing to leave Virginia behind. Once they had picked up Dillon from camp, they were to journey for two days, eventually meeting up with Elaine at their new home. She was traveling later that same day by plane, and would arrive before them.

"I expect you two to be good," Elaine said, buckling Lucy into her car seat. "Noah, that means you behave yourself and listen to Sarah. If you don't, I'll hear about it, and I won't be pleased."

Noah looked up and caught Sarah's gaze in the rear view mirror. She was frowning, yet something in her eyes made it seem as if she were trying to reassure him she wouldn't tattle. Noah nodded so she would know he understood. Sarah had never been anything but nice to him. He was more worried about Dillon.

"Drive safely, Sarah," Elaine said, taking a step away from the SUV, hand outstretched in a gesture of farewell. "I'll see you in a couple of days."

Sarah called out her goodbye, and backed the car down the drive. Pushing up as best he could, Noah twisted against the seatbelt, and watched out the back window as the only home he'd ever known grew smaller and smaller in the distance.

Frowning when they turned a corner and the house vanished completely, he wondered who would be bringing Midnight to their new place. Noah hadn't had the chance to go out and say goodbye to his colt. Surely Elaine must have arranged something. Midnight and all the other horses were part of their family, after all.

"Sarah, where are we going?" Noah had asked the question repeatedly of Elaine over the last few days. But for some reason his stepmother had seemed reluctant to answer, brushing aside his queries.

"We're going to your new home, Noah. In Texas."

Texas. That's where Elaine was from. All Noah knew of it was that it was far away and he thought cowboys, and possibly Indians, might live there.

They picked up Dillon halfway through their first day on the road. The older boy slipped in to the front passenger seat, put his Discman headphones over his ears, pulled his Gameboy out of his backpack and proceeded to ignore everything happening inside the car and out.

Noah didn't have anything to distract him, save for Lucy's childish babbling and the scenery rolling by on either side of the interstate. He watched as billboards and truck stops and farmland moved past his window, counted how many different kinds of license plates he could spy, and wondered what Texas would look like when they got there.

They spent the night east of someplace called Memphis at a motor lodge with a diner, but no swimming pool. Everyone was exhausted, with Lucy being especially cranky. Noah picked at the hamburger Sarah had ordered for him, but ate most of his French fries.

The room they were staying in had two big beds. Sarah and Lucy were sharing one; Dillon and Noah were sharing the other. When Sarah went into the bathroom with Lucy to get her ready for bed, Dillon said to Noah, "You kick me in your sleep and I'll make you regret it."

Dillon had brown hair and bright blue eyes, just like Lucy did. He was perhaps six inches taller than Noah and twenty pounds heavier. Noah felt certain he could make good on his threat.

"Okay," he said quietly.

Once in his pajamas, Noah climbed into bed, Tommy pressed to his chest, and scooted over as far as he could on his side of the mattress. He lay there very still, and listened to everyone else's breathing slow and deepen.

The next morning, he woke up exhausted, nearly nodding off over his oatmeal and orange juice. It was hard to sleep when you were afraid to move.

Sarah got them underway early. Sun poured through the car windows on Noah's side in a way it hadn't the day before. He closed his eyes against the glare, and drifted off to sleep.

By the time they stopped for lunch, he was feeling much more alert.

"We're in Texas, Noah," Sarah told him with a smile. "Can you believe it? It won't be long now."

It was actually several more hours before Sarah pulled off the highway onto a smaller county road and finally onto a private drive, marked by red brick pillars. The sun was beginning to fall to earth, casting long shadows. Everything around them was rolling and green, with stands of trees breaking up open meadows and fields abundant with crops.

"Here we are, everybody," Sarah said, when she came to the end of the drive. "Your new home."

Noah peered out the window and gasped at what he saw. The house was enormous, with two full floors of windows and another set of smaller windows above them, looking out from what he guessed must be an attic. It was painted a pale yellow with white trim, had a porch that ran across the front of it and down one side, and rounded columns at two of the corners that reminded Noah of towers in a castle. It looked old, but well-kept, as did the garage, and the stable beyond it. As everyone piled out of the car, stiff and sore from their journey, Elaine came out the front door to greet them.

"This is quite a place you've got here," Sarah called up to her as she circled around the SUV to release Lucy from her car seat.

Elaine smiled. "Six bedrooms, five baths, one hundred and fifty acres. It'll do."

As soon as Lucy was free, she scurried up the front steps to her mother. Elaine scooped her up into her arms and turned to go back inside. "Boys, help Sarah with the luggage."

There wasn't much to unload. They'd traveled light, with most of their belongings having been sent ahead with the movers. Noah had a duffle bag with a change of clothes, his pajamas, a toothbrush, and Tommy inside it. He hooked it over his shoulder and followed Sarah and Dillon inside.

The interior was as impressive as the exterior. Noah couldn't ever remember seeing his home in Virginia look this...perfect. A huge wooden staircase stood opposite the front door. On either side were what looked to be a large living room and a formal dining room. The hardwood floors and furniture gleamed, with everything seemingly new and fancier than what he was used to. Thick carpets with muted colors and intricate patterns were placed carefully to break up the spaces. Knickknacks and artwork were scattered about like jewels. Curious though he was, Noah was afraid to touch anything.

"Well, don't just stand there staring," Elaine said, Lucy still on her hip. "Take your things upstairs."

Lugging their bags, the travelers paraded up the stairs, Sarah in the lead, followed by Dillon and Noah, with Elaine and Lucy trailing behind.

When they got to the second floor, Elaine said, "Sarah, I have you in the guest room. It's the second door on the right. Why don't you get settled? Dillon, you're next door to Sarah at the end of the hall."

"Sweet," Dillon said, and elbowed past Sarah with his backpack, towards his room.

"Thanks," Sarah said. "Will you need me for anything right away?"

"I don't think so," Elaine said. "Take some time for yourself. Dinner will be in about an hour."

Sarah nodded and smiled, then took her bag into her room.

"What about me?" Noah asked. It had been a long day. And even though he wasn't a baby anymore, he thought maybe he'd like to take a nap before it was time to eat.

Elaine looked at him with a small, odd smile before saying, "You're upstairs."

Noah lifted his brows, surprised. But when Elaine gestured to a doorway through which he could see the stairs going up to another floor, he went without question. He'd thought there was only an attic up that high. But he guessed he must have been mistaken.

It wasn't until he got to the third floor that he realized Elaine hadn't come upstairs with him. She'd even closed the door at the bottom of the steps behind him. That was strange.

Still, looking around, it didn't seem as if he could get lost. There was a short hallway with only four doors. One door was open and clearly led to a small bathroom. Noah walked over to the door closest to him and opened it. Inside he saw what looked to be a storage room. Boxes were stacked from floor to ceiling along with a couple of trunks he had never seen before, and some other odds and ends. It was dusty inside the small room and smelled of moth balls and neglect. The late day sun slanted in through the small rectangular windows set deep within the eaves, painting boxes of light on the floor.

Confused, Noah went to the second room, across from the first. He opened it and found a small bedroom. The walls were painted a faded blue; white gauze curtains hung limp from the window opposite the door. There were no pictures hanging on the walls, nor decorations of any kind to be found. In the corner was a single bed with an iron headboard that had once been painted white, but over time had become chipped and worn, allowing the metal to show through from underneath. An ivory colored bedspread covered the mattress and a thin pillow. A battered nightstand stood beside the bed with a small lamp atop it. On the other side of the room was an equally shoddy dresser, missing a knob on one of the drawers. A small alcove with a wooden rod stood beside it. Hangars dangled from the pole like earrings. Noah guessed that was supposed to be some sort of closet.

Surely this couldn't be his room. Where was the furniture he'd had in the old house? His spaceman bedspread? Where were his things?

Fear beginning to churn in the pit of his stomach, Noah dropped his duffel on the floor by the bed and hurried to the last remaining room. This was the one Elaine meant to be his. Surely. This had to be it. He opened the door.

The room was already occupied.

The space was larger than the one he'd just left, with nicer furniture and a larger window. But what really set it apart from the other room was the hospital style bed against the far wall. In it lay a petite, frail-looking woman. Noah didn't recognize her at first. It had been weeks since he'd last seen her, and in that time she'd changed. Still, as soon as she turned her head on the pillow and looked his way, he could see her brown eyes held the same familiar warmth for him they always had. When the corner of her mouth lifted in a fragile smile, Noah couldn't restrain himself any longer.

"Grandma!" he cried, running from the doorway to her bedside. She lifted her hand from the lightweight blanket covering her. Noah grabbed hold of it in both of his, and held on tight. His grandmother didn't return the pressure. "Where have you been? I've missed you. How long have you been here? Why didn't you come back to the old house? Why do we have to live in Texas now? Can we go home? I don't think I like here."

In the past, whenever Noah had bombarded his grandmother with questions, she would always gently scold him, tell him to slow down and 'let me get a word in edgewise'. Now though, she didn't interject, didn't say a word. She just kept looking at him as if her eyes were hungry for the sight of him. Her hand began to tremble in his.

As he felt her shivering start, the joy humming through Noah at being reunited with his grandmother was silenced, concern instead rolling through him like a cloudbank. "Grandma...are you okay?"

She opened her mouth to speak, but no words came out at first. So, she licked her lips and tried again. And again. Noah watched as her efforts increased, until, swallowing hard, she was finally able to stutter out, "N-Noah."

Noah felt his eyes well with tears in a way they hadn't since his father had died. His grandma was hurt. And he didn't know what to do. "Grandma, w-what is it? What's wrong? Maybe I should get Elaine—"

His grandmother squeezed his hand. "No." She spoke the word louder and more easily than she had his name.

Blinking back his tears, Noah studied her face, trying to figure out what to do. Grandma looked older than the last time he'd seen her, thinner, more tired looking. And her face seemed...crooked. One side of her mouth appeared to be higher than the other.

That couldn't be right.

"Grandma, what should I do?" he whispered, frightened by how small she seemed, how weak. So different from the lively, confident woman who had ruled the roost in Virginia.

Her own eyes glistening now, his grandmother shook her head, her silver hair tangling on the pillow. "N-nothing."

Hoping to comfort them both, Noah toed off his shoes and curled up on the mattress beside his grandmother. Her bed was larger than the one across the hall. They fit easily. Noah rested his head on his grandmother's shoulder. It felt delicate beneath his cheek, like eggshells or a leaf after it had fallen from a tree.

"It's okay, Grandma," he told her, still holding her hand. "It's gonna be better now. You'll see. We're together. Don't worry. I'll take care of you."

He felt her tears dampen his hair before he heard her speak, her voice soft and halting. "S-sorry, Noah."

"Me too," he murmured just as quietly, finally allowing his own tears to fall. "Me too."

At his grandmother's urging, Noah went down for dinner when Elaine called. Dillon and Lucy were already at the table. Sarah hadn't come downstairs yet.

"Did you see your surprise?" Elaine asked him. She was watching him closely, but wasn't smiling at him. Noah couldn't decide just by looking at her whether she had thought it had been a good surprise for him or a bad one.

"When does my grandma get to eat?" he asked.

"Grandma?" Dillon said, looking up from his plate with surprise.

Elaine ignored her son. "You can take a plate up to her when you're finished."

Sarah's tread could be heard on the stairs. So any talk of surprises or the very sick woman upstairs was forgotten. Noah sat down to what looked like a delicious roast chicken dinner and ate without tasting much. Conversation went on around him, but he didn't contribute. The voices murmured like bees buzzing or the sound of rain tapping against a window pane. Background noise. His thoughts were far louder inside his head and consumed all his attention.

When the meal was finished, Elaine stood to begin collecting the dishes. "Sarah, would you mind taking Dillon and Lucy into the den. I thought it might be nice if we all sat down and watched a movie tonight. You three choose something. I need to talk to Noah for a minute."

Dillon and Lucy were already on their feet. Sarah hesitated for a moment, glancing in Noah's direction and frowning before saying, "All right. Come on, guys. Let's go figure out what we want to watch."

"Little Mermaid!" Lucy chanted, all but skipping out of the room. "Little Mermaid!"

"Shoot me," Dillon muttered as he followed behind.

Once they were alone, Elaine turned to look down at Noah, who was still seated at the table. "I'll put some food on a plate for you to take upstairs. When you're finished with it, I expect you to bring it back down here, clean it off, and put the dirty dish in the dishwasher."

"Yes, Ma'am," Noah said, his eyes flitting away to the napkin on his lap before meeting hers once more.

Studying Noah like he was a particularly fascinating variety of insect, Elaine was silent for a moment before she spoke again. "You know, Noah," she said, circling around the table to come closer to him. "Ever since your grandmother was released from the hospital, I've been paying a nurse to come in and look after her. But now that you're here, it occurs to me you might be able to do that instead."

Noah liked the idea of being able to help his grandmother. But he was just a little kid. What if he messed something up? "What would I have to do?"

Elaine shrugged. "See that she eats and takes her medicine. Help her get dressed, and get to and from the bathroom. That sort of thing. What do you think?"

Noah thought he could do what Elaine described. It seemed easy enough. And he really, really wanted to try. Only...

"But won't I be going to school soon?" he asked. He'd been so excited about going to kindergarten when the summer had started. Yet nobody had said anything about it since his father had died.

Elaine lifted her eyebrows. "You want to go to school rather than help your grandmother get better? Wow, Noah. That seems pretty selfish to me. I thought you loved her."

"I do love her," Noah said frowning, his heart beginning to race.

"It doesn't sound like it," Elaine said, shaking her head.

"No! I do," he said, pushing away from the table and to his feet, desperate suddenly to convince her of his interest. "I don't want to go. I want to stay with Grandma."

"Are you sure?"

"Yes."

Elaine gave it some thought. "And you would do everything I tell you to do?"

"Yes. Everything."

"You'd be good? You wouldn't be noisy or make messes, and you'd stay upstairs with your grandmother unless I specifically told you to come down?"

"Yes," Noah said with a nod. "Yes, I promise."

"Good boy," Elaine said. "Just remember, Noah, if you're bad or don't do a good job, I may have to send your grandmother away."

"No!" Noah said, his eyes welling at the thought. "Don't do that! Why would you send my grandma away?"

"For her own good," Elaine said. "She's a very sick woman. She needs someone to take care of her, someone who can be with her all the time. I can't do that. And a nurse is very expensive. Money doesn't grow on trees, you know."

"But I can do that," Noah insisted. "I told you. I promise I can."

Elaine hesitated for a moment before giving him a smile. "All right. I'll hold you to that. Now sit right there and I'll get you that food to take upstairs."

"Thank you," Noah said with a sigh, his heart rate easing. "Thank you, Elaine."

Elaine stopped halfway between the table and doorway. "Not Elaine, Noah. Don't forget, I'm your stepmother now."

The next morning, Noah came downstairs for breakfast. Sarah was already sitting at the dining room table, finishing her orange juice and cereal. Noah saw her suitcase sitting against the wall.

"Where are you going?" he asked, coming to stand beside her at the table.

Sarah smiled and turned towards him. "Back to Virginia, Noah."

"Could you take Grandma and me with you?" Noah asked, imagining for a moment how perfect it would be if it were only his grandmother and him again.

"I'm sorry, sweetheart, but no," she said. "You need to stay here with your mom and Dillon and Lucy."

Noah had a feeling she might answer that way. But he'd needed to try just the same. "Why do you have to go away?"

"I have to go back to school," Sarah said. "Classes started up at UVA last week. I'm already behind. But I'd wanted to make sure you guys got down here safely."

"I'll miss you," Noah said, feeling his eyes prickle with heat and wetness. He hadn't known Sarah long. But she had always been nice to him.

Sarah pulled him into her arms. "I'll miss you too."

"Isn't this touching?" Elaine said, coming into the dining room from the kitchen. "All ready to go, Sarah?"

"Yes, I think so," Sarah said, releasing Noah with a quick peck on his cheek. "All I need to do is toss my suitcase in the backseat, and I'm all set."

"I'm going to take Sarah to the airport, Noah," Elaine said. "Lucy will be going with me and Dillon is sleeping in. I've made up a plate for you to take upstairs. The nurse will be coming by around lunchtime to see your grandmother and show you what you need to do. I should be back by then."

That was a lot of information for Noah to take in all at once. He nodded and tried to keep it all straight. "All right."

"I'm going to go get Lucy ready," Elaine said. "I'll meet you outside."

Sarah nodded and watched as Elaine left the room. Then she turned to Noah. "Walk me to the car?" she asked, reaching down with one hand to pick up her suitcase and with the other to take Noah's hand.

"Okay," Noah said, smiling up at her. He figured it wouldn't hurt to spend a few more minutes with someone he liked and who seemed to like him back. Sarah had been a good friend to him. He didn't exactly have a lot of those around anymore.

Yet as they headed down the front steps, hand in hand, Noah saw something that took his mind off of Sarah and her impending departure.

"Midnight!"

Off in the corral next to the stable, the little horse was frolicking, while his mother, a big bay mare, watched from close by.

Noah let go of Sarah's hand and ran all the way to the pen. Even though he'd hoped he'd see Midnight again, Noah couldn't quite believe he was really there. He could tell Midnight was already growing, his frame filling out, his legs looking stronger. Noah recalled how he had promised his father he would look after his very special present, and felt ashamed he'd neglected Midnight so.

"I'm sorry, boy," he murmured as he watched Midnight trot around the ring. "I'm sorry I've been such a bad friend."

"I think I remember this little guy," Sarah said, coming to stand beside Noah at the fence. "Do you know his name?"

"His name is Midnight," Noah said, reaching out his hand in the hopes that Midnight might be coaxed to come over and be petted. "He's mine. I named him."

"He's yours?" Sarah said with surprise.

"Yeah," Noah said, smiling, delighted when the colt began cautiously making his way in Noah's direction. "My daddy gave him to me."

"You're one lucky boy, Noah," Sarah said quietly, watching as Noah petted Midnight gently on his muzzle in greeting.

Something in her voice drew Noah's eyes in her direction. "Do you think so?"

"Yeah, I do," she said. "I know it may not feel like it now, and that a lot of stuff has been really scary and confusing. But don't give up hope, okay? You're a good kid. I know there are going to be some pretty amazing things in store for you."

"How?" Noah said, frowning. "How do you know?"

"Because that's what you deserve," she said, smiling.

"Noah, come away from the horses!" Elaine called, coming down the porch stairs with Lucy in her arms. "We should get going, Sarah. You don't want to miss your flight."

"No, I don't," Sarah said, before turning to Noah. "Come on. We better listen to your mom."

Noah was still having trouble with that, thinking of Elaine as his stepmother. Still, he took Sarah's hand happily enough and walked back with her to the car.

"I guess this is it," Sarah said, bending down to wrap both her arms around him tight. Noah hugged her back. "You take care of yourself, and be a good boy. Listen to your mom."

"Good advice," Elaine said, standing on the other side of the car.

"Bye, Sarah," Noah said, trying to smile, though right at that moment he was having trouble remembering how.

"Bye, Noah," Sarah said as she got into the car.

"Noah, don't you have some things you need to attend to upstairs?" Elaine said, as she took her place behind the wheel.

Noah's eyes grew large. Grandma!

"Bye!" he said again with a wave, as he dashed up the front steps and in to the house.

He might be losing a friend with Sarah going back home. But he had gained two with Grandma and Midnight being there in

Texas with him. Now all he had to do was take care of them both.

Sarah might be right. Maybe there were going to be amazing things in store.

~*~*~*~

"Look at you—all gussied up for your first day at Louis T. Wigfall Junior High."

"Shut up, Cal," Matthew said as he waved to his mom and closed the front door behind him, his backpack slung over his shoulder. What was so 'gussied up' about new jeans and Nikes, and a striped oxford shirt?

"Sheesh. Some people just can't take a compliment," Cal said, dressed in his usual uniform of jeans, T-shirt and boots, his cowboy hat tipped back on his head.

There were days when Matthew had trouble remembering why Cal was his best friend. He loved the guy like a brother. But sometimes it seemed as if Cal's sole purpose in life was to ridicule everything Matthew said or did. While at the same time somehow supporting him. It was just weird the way he could do both so well.

"Yeah, well maybe I'd have an easier time taking a compliment if you got a little better at giving 'em," Matthew said, jogging around to the passenger side of Cal's pride and joy, a rebuilt 1985 Dodge Power Ram. The truck was cherry red and gleaming with its high buffed wax job. Matthew's dad's Mercedes might have cost more. But Matthew would have traded ten of those to own a truck like Cal's.

"Screw compliments," Cal said, watching Matthew from behind the wheel. "You want a ride or not?"

"I want," Matthew said, opening the truck's door and, after stowing his backpack on the floor of the cab, climbing inside.

"Don't we all, son. Don't we all," Cal said as he reached over and turned up the radio. With a twist of his wrist, Tim McGraw's latest ballad poured from the dashboard speakers.

Matthew had to admit, it was awfully nice of Cal to offer him a lift. His mom had said she would drive him, but it didn't take a genius to figure out that when you were twelve year-old boy, it was way cooler to be dropped off at school by your sixteen year-old truck-owning friend than by the president of the local women's auxiliary.

"So, are you excited?" Cal asked, pulling out of the circular drive in front of Matthew's home and onto the road leading to the county blacktop.

Matthew shrugged. "I guess."

"Who's in your homeroom again?"

Matthew thought about it for a second or two, the breeze blowing in through the open truck windows ruffling his hair. "Uh...let's see. Brad, Mike, Abby, Jenny, Kellie—"

"Kellie?" Cal echoed with a playful sideways glance. "You are so in there."

"In where?" Matthew said with a scowl.

"Did they not teach you basic anatomy in that fancy new elementary school you graduated from?" Cal teased.

"Cut it out," Matthew said, feeling the blush rising on his cheeks. "We're not like that, Kellie and me. We're friends. That's all."

Cal laughed. "All I'm saying is if you're looking for your first girlfriend, that little filly is a sure thing. She spent all summer watching you like you were USDA prime and she had a hankering for steak."

Matthew shook his head and glanced out the window. "You're so gross."

"I'm honest is what I am," Cal said, tapping along on the steering wheel now to Garth Brooks. "Come on, man, when I was your age I'd already started looking at girls. You can't be that different."

"Do not tell me you lost your virginity at twelve," Matthew said, vaguely horrified by the idea and the pressure that would be placed upon him if Cal had indeed been that precocious.

"Nah," Cal said. "I was a very mature thirteen."

"Oh, Lord."

"Yet fucked with the skill of a college man from what I've been told."

"Ew. I don't want to hear that! God—with the size of your ego, it's a mystery to me how there's room enough in this truck for the three of us," Matthew said, hoping his expression conveyed the proper measure of horror and dismay.

"You're not too rich for me to kick your ass to the curb, you know," Cal said with a growl that inspired nothing but affection in Matthew. "It's a couple miles out of my way to take you to Wigfall. My ego and I can go it alone."

"I could walk it."

"And scuff up those pretty new tennies? Please. Like I'd let you. Your momma would kill us both."

Smiling as he settled back in his seat to watch the countryside roll past, Matthew thought about what Cal had said. It wasn't the first time Cal had tried to talk to Matthew about the opposite sex, which was probably one of the disadvantages of having a best friend who was four years older than him. Cal took his role as adopted big brother very seriously.

Still, sometimes Matthew wondered if Cal wasn't only bringing up girls to brag and tease, if instead perhaps his friend could somehow sense the doubts Matthew had. About himself and what he did or did not find attractive.

Sure, Matthew liked girls. He liked them fine. They were nice to look at, softer than guys, and most of them smelled pretty good. He'd even kissed a couple at Abby's twelfth birthday party, when they'd played spin the bottle. It had gone okay, he guessed, once he had gotten over his worries about things like hamburger breath and where he should put his hands.

But being with a girl wasn't anything he actually yearned for or was anxious to try again. Not like Cal, who Matthew knew for a fact had felt up his babysitter, poor Penny Griggs, when he was only nine years old. Cal had thought it was hysterical and had boasted about it every chance he got until he hit puberty. Penny was in college now and probably scarred for life.

And sometimes...sometimes Matthew would notice something about a guy.

Like Luke, the college student his father had hired on that summer to help out with the garden. Luke was tall and had really broad shoulders and bright blues eyes that practically glowed from his deeply tanned face.

He'd been nice to Matthew when he'd seen him out on the property. He would make a point of saying hello and chatting with him about school or the Cowboys' chances that season or whatever. Matthew had liked that. Luke had talked to him like an adult, man to man. And if, as they'd spoken, Matthew had noticed things like how strong Luke's hands had seemed or the way the muscles in his arms had flowed under his skin when he gestured, well...Matthew was just observant that way. That was all.

At least...that was what Matthew thought might be the reason. He couldn't be sure.

And until he was, he couldn't really talk about it with anyone.

Not even someone as close to him as Cal.

At first, Noah didn't really mind living in Texas as much as he'd feared he might.

It was lonely, sure. He didn't ever leave the property, so he never met anyone new, save for the people who helped Elaine with things like the horses and the landscaping.

The gardeners were Mexican and didn't speak English very well. So he didn't make any friends there. They would smile at him, but left Noah alone. He tended to do the same.

The man in charge of the stable was named Willis. Noah didn't know if that was his first name or his last. He wasn't a terribly big man; Noah didn't think he was as tall as his father had been. Willis wasn't particularly heavy either. But he seemed plenty strong. Noah had seen him lifting bales of hay and shoveling out the stalls, and knew while Willis didn't look like a muscleman, he also didn't have any trouble doing that kind of work.

Willis scared Noah some. He had thick black hair and dark hooded eyes, and a face that seemed set in a permanent scowl. He smelled of cigarettes and sweat. When Noah would see Willis on his trips to visit Midnight, the stable hand never really said much. He just looked at Noah like he wished Noah would disappear.

Noah wished he was brave enough to tell Willis the feeling was mutual.

Still, for the most part, he was able to stay out of Willis' way. Noah tended to spend most of his days indoors. The nurse who had been looking after his grandmother before Noah had arrived had shown Noah early on what he could do to help. He had learned how best to get his grandmother from her bed to her feet, how to help her get dressed and get into and out of their bathroom's tiny shower.

He how learned what pills she needed to take and how often, and how to do the exercises with her that would help improve her speech and strength.

He knew the nurse thought showing these kinds of things to a little boy was a waste of time.

"I'm afraid he's not going to have the coordination or upper body strength to do what needs to be done," she had said to Elaine, who had been present to watch the demonstration. "Besides—how is he going to remember everything?"

"Oh, don't worry," Elaine had said, her charm out in full force. "I'll be here to supervise. Noah just wants to help."

Only once the nurse was gone, Elaine never went anywhere near Noah's grandmother. She was willing to provide food and other essentials like clothing or linens if asked. She'd even agreed to put a television in the room and allowed Noah to bring upstairs books from the first floor library. But she never set foot on the third floor herself. That belonged to Noah and his grandmother. As Grandma would never be able to make it to the first floor on her own, everything depended on Noah. So he tried his best to stop worrying about making mistakes and instead just do what needed to be done.

Over time, Grandma became stronger, though she would never be the vital woman she once had been. She tired easily, took naps every day and sometimes she didn't remember things as well as she used to. Still, using her walker, she was grew able to shuffle to and from the bathroom with little assistance, her speech improved, and she was finally able to spend her days not in her bed, but in the corner reading chair instead.

It was from there that she tutored Noah in his studies.

"You have to go to school," she'd said to him when Noah had told her he would be spending his days with her instead.

"You need me more," Noah had said. "Please, Grandma. Don't send me away. I want to be here with you."

Brow wrinkled with worry, his grandmother had reluctantly agreed. "All right, sweetheart. For now."

At first, they'd focused on simple things like the difference between consonants and vowels, and learning the numbers from zero to one hundred, the kinds of things he would be learning if he'd gone to kindergarten.

"You'll need to know this," Grandma had said, her words slurring some, but not so much that Noah couldn't understand her. "For first grade."

But when a year had passed, and Noah had seemed no more likely to leave the third floor and go off to school as Dillon and even Lucy now had done, Grandma had stopped talking about school and begun broadening what she was teaching him instead.

She started showing Noah how to read, and add and subtract. Together they would pore over the thick atlas Noah had found downstairs, and his grandmother would point out where Texas was on the map and quiz him on all fifty states and their capitols. For his part, Noah looked forward to the lessons. Grandma was patient with him, and generous with her praise. Learning in this way added structure and focus to his days. He didn't miss regular school at all, even if he did sometimes miss playing with children his own age.

Yet not all his time was spent upstairs with his grandmother. Elaine began to find other things for him to do as well.

"It isn't good for a growing boy like you to sit idle all day," she told him when she called him downstairs one morning. "It seems to me there are other ways you can be useful."

So Noah began to be assigned chores.

At first, Elaine asked him to sweep outside, on the front porch and walks.

"I want our home to look welcoming, Noah. So make sure you shake out the mats while you're at it."

Then, she asked him to do similar work indoors.

"There's no reason why you can't push a vacuum and a mop. You're a strong boy. Put your back into it."

Gradually, over time, she came up with other projects— taking out the garbage, dusting, cleaning the bathrooms.

"Noah," his grandmother said to him one day, when he came back upstairs after working that morning for Elaine. "Come here, son."

Noah smiled and went to perch on the ottoman in front of her chair. It felt good to sit down for a minute.

"Let me see your hands."

Puzzled, he extended them, palms down. His grandmother took them gently in hers. Noah could feel the slight tremble in her touch that he couldn't really see, but he knew had never entirely gone away.

Saying nothing at first, she ran her fingers slowly down the length of his hands, gliding from the heel to his fingertips. "They're rough," she said after a moment. "I can almost feel the lines."

Noah was strangely embarrassed. "I can go wash them," he said, pulling free.

Before he could stand, she stopped him. "No, honey. No. That's not... She works you hard, doesn't she?"

Noah didn't want his grandmother to worry. Not ever. She had enough to concern herself about without fearing for him. So he fibbed. Just a little. "Sometimes. But I don't mind."

His grandmother looked at him as if she didn't quite believe him. "You don't?"

"No," he said. "I like to be busy."

She studied his face for a few seconds more before shaking her head. "Noah, you're so much like your father."

"I am?" he asked, brightening.

"Yes," she said. "He always tried to protect the people he loved."

Noah beamed. His daddy had been a great man. Grandma saying Noah was like him was the best compliment he'd ever received.

Grandma smiled back at him. But her eyes were sad. "I don't

want that, you know."

Noah cocked his head, confused. "Don't want what?"

"For you to sacrifice yourself. Not for me."

Noah didn't know what to say to that. So he settled on the one thing he knew he could always count on to make his grandmother happy. "I love you, Grandma."

Only it didn't seem to work this time. Her smile faltered and her eyes got shiny. "I know you do. Just promise me you won't let her use that against you."

Noah wasn't entirely sure what Grandma meant by that, but he knew she was talking about Elaine.

Late one Saturday morning the summer Noah turned eight, he was in the kitchen, sweeping, trying to decide what he would do once he was finished. He'd been working around the house since just after dawn, but this was the last of it. And while his grandmother kept his lessons going year-round, she gave him weekends off. So the rest of the day would be his to do with as he liked.

The bowl of apples serving as a centerpiece on the kitchen table helped him decide. He would visit Midnight.

He tried to get out to see his horse as often as he could, but sometimes days would pass before he could find time to go to the stable, and he was almost never able to bring along a treat. Elaine had strictly forbidden him from going into the kitchen cabinets or the refrigerator. The apples, however, were out in plain sight. So Noah felt fairly confident the usual rules didn't apply. Just to be safe, he chose a small one, tucked it into the pocket of jeans and pulled his T-shirt over the resulting bulge. It didn't entirely camouflage the lump. But with his work winding down, Elaine had retired to her office to answer some correspondence. Noah thought he could probably get out the front door without her noticing. Never had he been so thankful for Dillon's oversized hand-me-downs.

Stowing the dustpan and broom, he made his getaway. It was bright in the yard, the August sun overhead huge and blazing.

Noah missed the air-conditioned comfort to be found inside the house. Still, all heat and sweat were soon forgotten when he saw his horse in the corral, trotting around its circumference, its halter in place.

"Midnight!" Noah called, running towards him.

Hearing Noah's voice, Midnight's ears pricked and his head turned. By the time Noah had reached the pen, the horse was waiting for him at the side of the pen.

"Hi, boy," Noah said, climbing up and sitting on the corral's top rail, so he could reach over and pat Midnight's cheek. "I brought you a surprise." Reaching into his pants pocket, he dug out the apple and held it out to Midnight, who took it with great delicacy and crunched it down, core and all. Noah watched him eat it, delighted.

"You're getting so big," Noah said, running his hand along the stallion's sleek, muscled neck. "I think you're even taller than your momma now. I'll bet you're faster than her too with those long legs. I've seen you sometimes, playing in the corral with the other horses and you can outrun all of them."

Midnight seemed to take the praise as his due, nudging Noah as if looking for more attention, or perhaps just another apple. Noah could only laugh, squirming with happiness.

"Hey, kid. What are you doing there?"

Noah looked over from his seat on the rail and saw Willis coming towards him, carrying an armload of tack. As always, the stable hand made Noah nervous, but he held his ground.

"Nothing. I'm just saying hi to Midnight."

Willis dumped the equipment he was carrying beside a post positioned near the middle of the pen. His hands empty, he then circled wide to come up alongside Midnight and take hold of his halter. "Well, beat it. Your friend and I have some work to do."

Noah didn't want Willis anywhere near Midnight, which he knew was silly, as Willis was the one who took care of everyone's horses, and they all seemed to be doing well. Still, something about Willis bothered Noah. He didn't trust him, especially not with anything as precious as Midnight. "What are you going to do?"

"Nothing that's any of your business. Go back in the house."

"I want to watch," Noah said, determined not to back down. He had told his father he was going to look out for Midnight and that was what he intended to do.

"I said get out of here!" With his free hand, Willis reached out and shoved Noah hard, nearly unseating him from his perch atop the corral. "Go on. Get! Before I tell your mother on you."

Noah clung like a monkey to the rough wooden rail, saving himself from falling backwards, but winding up with a palm full of splinters as a result.

"Hey!" he yelped, as he rolled down and to his feet, his wounded hand cradled against his chest.

Willis only looked at him and smirked before turning his attention once more towards Midnight.

Noah stood beside the pen, hesitating for a second longer. But he knew, if he didn't do as he'd been told, Willis would indeed follow through on his threat. Elaine liked and trusted the stable hand. There wasn't a chance in the world she would take Noah's side over his. With a sigh, Noah began walking back towards the house, pausing often to look over his shoulder and see what Willis was up to.

At first, everything seemed to be fine. Willis led Midnight over to where he'd dropped the mound of equipment. Taking the rope lead that was tied there, he clipped the horse to the post to keep him near and began fitting him with a bridle. Once that was in place, Willis turned and picked up a pad Noah knew was normally placed beneath a saddle.

Noah was aware Willis had been working with Midnight since the horse had been very young. Just that week, he had seen Willis leading the horse in a circle around the pen, getting him to go from a walk to a trot to a canter just by saying the command. But he had never seen the stable hand try and put a saddle on Midnight before. That had Noah worried.

With Willis' attention firmly on his work, Noah took the opportunity to duck beside an ancient hickory tree that grew halfway between the stable and house. Its thick trunk provided him an excellent hiding place from where he could watch what was happening with his horse.

Midnight seemed to tolerate the bridle well enough. But he didn't like when Willis began to lay things on top of him. The moment the pad was draped across the center of his back, Midnight edged sideways, pulling at the lead. When Willis placed the saddle on top of that, Midnight grew unhappier still, tossing his head and making small sounds of distress.

Noah dug his fingers into the bark of the tree, trying to hold himself back from running to the rescue. "Stop it," he murmured to Willis under his breath. "Stop it right now."

Only Willis didn't stop. He moved with the horse, determined to secure the saddle in place.

"You listen to me, you stubborn son of a bitch," Willis growled, wrestling with the girth's buckle, while Midnight pranced and swayed. "Don't you puff up your stomach on me, boy. I'm on to your tricks. You stand here now and you take this, or so help me God I will take my boot and I will shove it up your spoiled rotten ass."

Oh no, Noah thought. That was enough of that.

"Leave him alone!" he yelled, running full tilt from his hiding place towards the corral.

Taken off guard by Noah's impassioned cry, Willis turned to look at him, forgetting for a moment he had over a thousand pounds of agitated stallion stirring beside him.

Midnight, who had already been unsettled before Noah's shout, became even more upset after the outburst. His dark eyes rolling, the horse whinnied and spun, kicking out with his hind legs.

No stranger to horses, Willis recognized the danger, but was a second too late. Before he could get himself clear, one of Midnight's hooves clipped him in the knee.

"Christ!" Willis screamed, crumpling, holding his leg and rolling swiftly beyond Midnight's reach.

By the time Willis had been struck, Noah had arrived at the pen, horrified by what had occurred, his eyes like pie plates, his mouth opening and closing mutely, all words beyond him.

"What did you do?" Willis grunted as he climbed unsteadily to his feet. "What the fucking hell did you do?"

Noah wet his lips before he spoke. "You...y-you were hurting him."

"You stupid little shit," Willis said, his voice gravelly and low, advancing on Noah slowly but steadily, his gait uneven and painful looking. "I wasn't fucking hurting him. I've been doing this for more than twenty years. I think I know enough not to hurt the God damned livestock."

Noah stood there paralyzed, everything inside him urging him to run, yet at the same time he knew there wasn't really anyplace he could hide. "I'm s-sorry. I-I didn't know—"

"You didn't know?" Willis echoed, hand on the corral's top rail to help support himself as he made his way to the gate. "You didn't know you could have killed me, you mean? What if that horse had kicked me in the head instead of the leg, huh? What if he'd trampled me?"

Noah shook his head and inched away. "I didn't mean—"

"Oh, yeah?" Willis said, exiting the pen. "Well that's the difference between you and me, kid. Because this? This is definitely something I mean." Moving as a fast as a snake striking its prey, he reached out and, with a hard, flat hand, slapped Noah across the face.

The blow was enough to send Noah to the dirt. He landed on his hip with a choked wordless cry.

"You want more of that, kid? Huh?" Willis said, looming over him. "Or would you rather tell me again how to do my job?"

"No," Noah said, scrambling backwards in the dirt, trying desperately to get to his feet. Only he was trembling so hard, he couldn't seem to get his body to work. Tears were blinding him, and he could taste blood where Willis's hand had caught the corner of his mouth, splitting his lip.

"What is going on here?"

Noah turned his head and saw Elaine coming down the front steps, all but glowing in her summer whites. She looked cool and perfect as always, and Noah had never felt like more a mess.

"Your boy here tried to kill me," Willis said as Elaine drew near.

"That's not true!" Noah said, at long last struggling to his feet. "I was trying to keep him from hurting my horse."

"Your horse?" Elaine said, arching her brow. "Don't be ridiculous, Noah. You don't have a horse."

"Yes, I do!" Noah said, pointing towards the corral. "Midnight is mine."

"Midnight most certainly is not yours," Elaine informed him with a maddeningly degree of calm. "Once he's ready, I'll probably give him to Dillon to ride. But at the end of the day, all the horses, like everything else on this property, belong to me."

Utter disbelief made Noah reckless. "No! That's...*no*! My daddy gave me Midnight for my birthday. He belongs to me. Not you. You can't give him to Dillon. You can't give him to anybody. Nobody should be allowed to ride him but me."

His outburst seemed to break through some of Elaine's typical reserve. "You ungrateful little brat," she said, stepping closer to him, her hands on her hips, her eyes narrowing. "I allow you and your grandmother to live here. Provide you with food and shelter and the clothes on your back. And this is how you repay me—by raising your voice to me and telling me what I can and cannot do?"

Noah had never heard that tone of voice from Elaine before. In the past, whenever she'd gotten irritated with him, her cool had simply gotten colder. She might mock, she might give him additional chores, but she'd never let him see her angry.

She was angry now.

Noah found it kind of terrifying.

"What if I decide to get rid of that horse entirely?" she asked with a smile that made the hair on the back of Noah's neck stand on end. "I could sell him, you know, or tell Willis here to put a bullet in his head. And no one could stop me. Legally, he's my property."

"No!" Noah said, reaching out as if he could physically keep her from doing what she threatened. "No, please..."

"Would that make you feel better, Noah?" Elaine asked. "That way no one would ever ride him. Would that make you happy?"

"No," Noah said, shaking his head. "No, no, no, no, no."

Elaine said nothing for a moment, as if she were weighing what exactly to do next. Finally, she nodded. "All right then. See that you remember that."

Noah looked down at his feet. He could feel tears welling and he didn't want her to see them. "Yes, Ma'am."

"Go up to your room and stay there. I'll call you down when dinner is ready and you can take a tray upstairs to your grandmother. You, however, will be going without tonight."

Sighing, Noah nodded, and started on his way. It wasn't the first time he had gone without a meal as punishment, but going hungry was never any fun.

Before he could make it all the way inside, he heard Elaine call out from behind him. "Oh, and Noah—one more thing."

Noah turned around to look at her. Her face was wiped clean of all expression. Willis was standing beside her however with an ugly smile. "Yeah?"

"Unless you're given specific permission from either Willis or me, don't go anywhere near Midnight again."

"But, why can't--?"

"Do you really want to challenge me on this, Noah?"

Blinking back tears, Noah shook his head again and went inside.

He wanted to challenge all kinds of things. But he feared the consequences if he were to disobey.

"Please don't hate me."

"What makes you think I do?"

"I'd hate me if I were you."

"Good thing I'm a better person than you are, then."

"Yeah. Good thing."

It had to be after three. The sky was pitch black overhead save for the layer of stars dusted over it, like sugar spilled on an ebony tablecloth. His parents had turned in hours ago, after most of the party guests had headed home. They'd invited quite a crowd to celebrate Matthew's high school graduation. He would guess more than half the county had shown up to eat, drink and dance until the wee hours of the morning. Only a few diehards, all friends of Matthew, still remained. And most of them were either passed out or making out. Matthew had plenty of privacy.

Which was why he'd thought no one would notice if he snuck off into the pool house with Charlie to fool around a little.

He hadn't counted on Cal seeking him out to say goodbye.

"Were you ever planning on telling me?" Cal asked now, taking a sip of his beer. They were sitting on the flatbed of his truck, surrounded by his band's speakers, mikes and other equipment, their legs dangling off the open tailgate.

Matthew scratched at the label on his beer with his thumbnail. He didn't look at his friend. "Eventually."

"Like when? When you asked me and the guys to play at your big gay wedding? I should warn you—we charge more for weddings than we do graduations. The happy couple almost always makes us play the fucking hokey-pokey. It's only fair we get compensated for it."

"Please. Like I'd marry Charlie."

"Thank God. That boy is an even bigger twink than you are."

That made Matthew glance in Cal's direction. Cal was smirking at him. "You know what a twink is?"

"Son, when are you gonna realize that not only am I older and better looking than you are, but I'm way smarter."

Matthew shook his head and looked away. "Yeah, well...right now you don't exactly need to convince me of that."

Cal stretched out his foot and gently tapped one of his cowboy boots against Matthew's leg. "There's no need to be so hard on yourself, you know. This doesn't change anything."

Matthew met Cal's eyes. He didn't see anything in them that looked angry or disgusted. Something that had been squeezing Matthew's heart eased up on its grip. "You're sure?"

"Yeah, I'm sure. You're my friend." Cal said it like that was all the explanation necessary.

Sometimes Matthew really loved the guy.

"Thanks."

"You're welcome."

Neither of them said anything for a moment, each content to enjoy the soft evening air and sip their beer. Finally, Cal broke the silence. "You said anything to your parents yet?"

Matthew shook his head. "Nah. I just... I'm not really sure

myself, you know? What if this is just some sort of phase? I'd hate to get them all worked up over nothing."

"Is that what you think this is?" Cal said. "Something you're going to outgrow?"

"I don't know," Matthew said, having asked that same question himself the past couple of years. "It would be easier for everybody if it were."

"So easy is what you want?" Cal asked, though really it sounded like more of a statement.

Frowning, Matthew glanced down at his hands and shrugged.

"'Cause it seems to me that truth is way better than easy," Cal said. "You know what I mean?"

Matthew chuckled and looked Cal's way. "I don't get you, man. Why aren't you freaking out about this?"

"Is there something I should be freaking out about?" Cal asked. "I mean—you're not after my ass, right?"

"No!" Matthew practically yelped. "God, no."

"Thanks, Matt," Cal said with a wry smile. "That's reassuring."

Feeling on more solid ground, Matthew teased, "I could make a play for you if you think it would make you feel better."

"I appreciate the offer," Cal said, his smile widening. "But I think I'm good."

Matthew lifted his beer in a mock toast and took another sip.

"No, it's just...you and the people you want to sleep with..." Cal said, clearly searching for the proper words, "none of that affects you and me, you know?"

Matthew nodded. He did know. Now, anyway. "Were you surprised?"

"Would you be upset if I say no?"

"Really?" Matthew asked, not upset, but a bit surprised himself. "You thought I went for guys?"

"I thought you didn't get all that excited about girls," Cal said. "There's a difference."

Matthew had to admit—Cal wasn't wrong. He'd done what he was supposed to do all through high school. He'd gone to the barbeques and the school dances. He'd flirted and dated, and never lacked for female interest or company. Yet, while he honestly liked many of the girls he'd gone out with and had even enjoyed most of the things they'd done together physically, he always knew something else—something important—was missing.

"I feel like I've been playing a role," he confessed. "Like part of me needs to keep playing it. I'm the only kid my parents have, and they've invested a lot in me—a lot of time, a lot of money and a lot of energy. I don't want to let them down."

"Matthew, your parents love you," Cal said, putting his beer aside to make his point. "All they care about is you being safe and happy."

"Yeah, well trust me—as far as they're concerned, there's no way their son will ever find happiness with another guy," Matthew said. "That's just not the way their world works."

Cal shook his head. "I know you like to be the perfect son. But sometimes it's got to be about what you want, not what your parents want. Otherwise you'll only end up resenting the people you're trying so hard to be perfect for. That's no way to live."

"No, I know," Matthew said, nodding. "And I promise, once I figure out...what I need to figure out, I'll talk to them. Just...not yet."

Cal studied him for a moment before bobbing his head in agreement. "Yeah, all right. You'll be a big ol' college man soon. Being down in Austin will give you some breathing room. You find an apartment yet?"

"No, not yet," Matthew said. "My dad is after me to just move to our place on the lake, but I think I'd like something closer to campus."

"Only you would turn down the chance at a luxury lakefront mansion to live in a noisy, overcrowded rat trap near UT."

"You live in a noisy, overcrowded rat trap near UT."

"Yeah, but I'm a starving musician," Cal said. "Besides, I'm usually the one making the noise."

Matthew laughed, as he knew Cal had wanted him to. Cal just watched him, a faint smile on his face, and finished up the last of his beer. Matthew finally asked, "Are we good, man?"

"Yeah." Cal nodded. "We're good."

Matthew smiled and reached out to clap Cal on the shoulder.

He hadn't exactly planned on coming out to his best friend that night. But it could have gone worse than it did.

Now all Matthew had to do was decide what he wanted. That shouldn't be so hard.

He was pretty sure he'd know it when he saw it.

At fourteen, Noah hated his life. He hadn't been all that happy with it prior to fourteen, of course. But once puberty had hit, as solid as one of Willis' increasingly frequent slaps, everything got just that much worse.

Noah had shot up six inches in the last year. Sometimes when he fell into bed at night, so exhausted he couldn't even keep his eyes open, his aching joints would stop him from falling asleep.

Yet his weight hadn't quite caught up with his growth spurt, so when he looked in the mirror, the guy looking back at him was gawky and awkward, all elbows and knees and feet. The clothes handed down to him from the more solidly built Dillon hung off him. His stepbrother delighted in calling him Scarecrow. And much worse.

Adding some inches was one thing. But his body was rebelling in other ways too. His skin had started breaking out and his voice had developed the habit of cracking without reason or warning.

But worst of all was what was going on inside, the restlessness he could feel stirring like a serpent, distracting and dangerous. A restlessness it was impossible to do anything about, given the way he lived.

Over the last few years, his routine had changed. Ever since his confrontation with Willis, Elaine had decided it might be better if Noah spent more time working under the stable hand's direction.

"Willis has told me he could use some help," she'd said with a smile Noah had come to distrust. "You like horses, Noah. I'm sure you'll learn a lot working for him."

What Noah had learned was how gross it was mucking out stalls. Willis had plenty of work for him to do, all of it backbreaking and guaranteed to make Noah not only filthy, but stink. He shoveled manure, swept and mopped the stable floor, pitched hay, made sure all of Elaine's horses were fed and watered, and that their tack was well maintained. And when Noah's work inside the stable was complete, there was always more to do outside or in the house. Lessons with his grandmother had all but ceased. He was lucky if he could find the energy in the evenings to sit with her for a couple of hours and watch some television before bed.

Through it all, Willis watched him like a hawk, quick to find fault, and fond of disciplining with a slap or a push. The first time he'd backhanded Noah for a mistake, Noah had threatened to bring such treatment to Elaine's attention. Willis had only laughed.

"Your stepmother told me to do what I felt was necessary to keep you in line, boy," Willis had said with a grin. "Go right ahead and tell her. See what it gets you."

What it had gotten him was no dinner that night.

"Some boys need a firm hand," Elaine had said when Noah told her of Willis' abuse. "I trust Willis to know what's best. Don't come to me telling tales, Noah. I don't want to hear them. Especially not from you."

Yet not everyone turned a blind eye. Noah's grandmother had noticed the changes and voiced her concern. "It's not right for a boy your age to work so hard."

"It's okay, Grandma," Noah had assured her, not wanting her to worry. "I'm just doing chores. It's only...now that I'm older, I can take on more. That's all. I'll bet lots of boys help out with this kind of stuff."

In reality, he could only guess at what 'lots of boys' did. He wasn't really certain. In all his years of living in Texas, Noah had still never set foot off the property.

How could he? Where would he go?

He didn't attend school. He didn't know how to drive. He didn't even know what lay beyond the horizon. No matter in what direction he looked, everything he saw belonged to Elaine.

She wouldn't let him anywhere near the phone. The computer was password protected. Either Elaine or Willis were present whenever he was working. And anytime people came to the house, he was sent upstairs to sit with his grandmother. Together, they were trapped, like virtual prisoners.

Besides, even if he were able to tell someone about the way they lived, what could he say? He had his own room, he was fed (most of the time), had clothes to wear, and while Willis' blows hurt, they rarely left marks. In the end, it would be Elaine's word against that of his grandmother and him. Given what Noah had seen of her over the years, he had little doubt his stepmother would be able to talk her way out of any potential trouble. After all, Elaine was a respected widow and mother, a pillar of the community. He was just her ragamuffin stepson.

But that didn't mean he never dreamed of escape.

Late at night, he would lie in his narrow bed and stare at the shadowed ceiling overhead, imagining what it would be like to be on his own. The idea of freedom, sweet and virtually unknown, beckoned, so very tempting.

Only leaving Elaine's house would mean leaving his grandmother behind. Noah didn't see how he would ever be able to do that. She still counted on him for so much. Elaine would never be able to show her the love and care that Noah could. And what if Elaine punished her for Noah running away by neglecting her or hurting her in some way? His grandmother was still so frail; she would never be able to protect herself.

"No," Noah whispered one night, lying on his stomach, his arms wrapped around his pillow, hugging it close. It was okay to dream about running away. But he would never be able to actually do it. Not until he was grown up and had a way to take care of his grandmother and himself. There was too much risk any other way.

"I can stick it out," he murmured to Tommy, who still hung around, his once white fur nearly gray now, one of his button eyes hanging loose on its thread. "I just need to wait until the time is right, until I can find someone I can trust, someone who will help me get Grandma out of here."

Tommy looked back at him, unblinking, from where he was propped against the bedside lamp.

Tired though he was, and filled with all kinds of nameless concerns, Noah had to smile. At himself and the "person" he was talking to. "You know...you were a much better friend when I was five than you are now."

Half cloaked by night, Tommy smiled back at him, as mysterious and enduring as a sphinx.

~*~*~*~

Late July tended to be brutal in Texas. At least that was Noah's experience. Scorching hot sun, dry air that was almost painful to breathe and little wind. The dog days of summer were when he most missed working indoors. Thank God his grandmother could take advantage of the house's central air conditioning, even if he couldn't. He was looking forward to taking a shower when he was done for the day with an almost physical ache.

At least that morning he was working in the shade. Willis had him inside the stable, mucking out the stalls. And he was on his own. For a few minutes anyway.

"Listen, boy. I've gotta go up to the house and have a little chat with your stepmom. I won't be gone long, and when I get back, you better damn well have those stalls cleaned out and fresh hay put in the feeders. You understand me?"

"Yes, Sir."

Noah would have agreed to anything if it got Willis off his back.

With the heat being what it was, he was stripped down to a white sleeveless T-shirt over a threadbare pair of jeans he'd cut off just above the knees. As with most of his clothes, neither fit him well. But Noah had taken a piece of rope he'd found in the tack room and fashioned it into a belt to hold the pants up. On his feet was a pair of Dillon's old gym shoes. They were also too big for him. So Noah wore thick white socks to help keep them from falling off. He had a blue bandana tied around his hairline to keep the sweat from his eyes.

He was in one of the middle stalls, humming quietly to himself as he used a pitchfork to scoop away the dirty straw, when he heard a funny noise. It sounded like a horse's hooves thudding against the ground, but he didn't see how that was possible. All the horses were in their stalls with the exception of Marigold, Lucy's mare. Noah had tied her up just outside while he cleaned her space. Leaning his pitchfork against the stall's wall, he went out to investigate.

What he saw when he stepped outside took his breath away.

Thundering towards him on a muscular brown and white pinto was the most handsome man Noah had ever seen. He had on a grey T-shirt, jeans, and boots. Nothing special, but he wore it very well. He rode his horse like he'd been born in a saddle, moving with it smoothly and easily. It was hard to tell with him being seated, but Noah thought he was probably about as tall as Noah was himself. His shoulders were broad and his waist was narrow. His hair was shorter and lighter-colored than Noah's shaggy mop, shining nearly gold in the sunlight. He looked like something out of a magazine. Like something out of a movie.

And all at once, Noah was reminded of his own appearance and the fact that he'd spent the last hour shoving horseshit.

He wondered if it was too late to hide.

"Hi," said the horseman as he trotted up to Noah and reined the pinto to a stop.

Apparently hiding was out of the question.

"Hey," Noah replied, gazing up at him. Now that he could get a better look at the guy, Noah realized he was almost more a boy than a man, and probably only a few years older than him. He could also see the stranger was even handsomer than Noah had first thought. He had freckles dusted across his cheeks and nose, and the bluest eyes Noah had ever seen.

"I'm looking for Elaine," the guy said, startling Noah out of his musings. In a smooth move Noah knew he would never have been able to pull off, the visitor then swung his right leg over the saddle and half-slid, half-jumped to the ground on the left side of his horse, landing lightly, all the while hanging on to the reins.

"Ah. Well...um, she's probably up at the house," Noah said, thinking to himself as he spoke that this was the first time in nearly ten years he'd talked to someone who wasn't a family member or Willis. Part of him would have given anything to be a little more articulate.

Part of him was surprised he was able to get out any words at all.

"Oh, good," the guy said with a smile Noah found as attractive as every other aspect of him. "I was afraid I had the wrong place. I'd told my mom I'd ride over here instead of driving, but then I realized about halfway here I wasn't really sure how to come this way. I was afraid I was gonna get lost."

Noah grinned back at him, helpless to do anything else. "Nah. You're in the right place."

His smile dimming just a touch, the guy hesitated for a moment, like he was surprised by something. Then he seemed to shake himself, smiled more broadly and extended his hand. "I should probably introduce myself. I'm Matthew. My folks own Valley View a couple of spreads west of here."

Noah didn't know Valley View. But it sounded nice. He pulled off his work gloves and tucked them in his back pocket before taking Matthew's hand in his. "Hi. I'm Noah."

"Hey, Noah," Matthew said, giving Noah's hand a firm shake

before releasing it. "So, is it okay if I head on up to the house? I'm supposed to pick up a check for my mom. It's something for the women's auxiliary fashion show... I don't know. She said Elaine would have it ready for me."

"Oh! Sure. Yeah. Um...come on, this way," Noah said, gesturing in the general direction of the house.

"Is there someplace I can tie up The Bean here? Maybe get him some water?" Matthew said, glancing over at his horse, whose coat was shiny and wet with sweat.

"Oh, yeah," Noah said. "That's not a problem. The trough is around the side here. I can take him if you want."

"Would you? Oh man, that would be great. Thanks," Matthew said, handing him the reins. "It's so hot today; I probably shouldn't even have ridden him. I just know I'm gonna miss him when I go away to school. So, I'm trying to get in all the rides I can."

"Where are you going?" Noah asked as they fell in together, walking side by side.

"UT," Matthew said. "I'm only here another month or so, then I'm gone."

For some ridiculous reason, the news that Matthew would be leaving soon made something heavy and hard form at the base of Noah's throat, a weight he had trouble swallowing past. It was stupid, of course, he told himself. It wasn't as if they were friends. It made no sense to mourn something he'd never had.

Shaking his head at his own silliness, Noah put a determined smile on his face and led them to the trough, where he looped the pinto's reins around the post there. "So, did I hear you say your horse was called The Bean?"

Matthew chuckled and looked down at the ground, his hand coming up to rub over the back of his neck. "Yeah. You know— pinto? Bean? It was funny when I was twelve."

Noah shrugged, his smile lingering. "It's funny now."

Matthew looked up again, meeting Noah's eyes, his own gaze amused. "I have a feeling you're a forgiving audience."

Noah nodded. "Most of the time."

"Hey, Matthew!"

Noah looked over and saw Dillon all but running towards the

stable. Behind him, Noah could make out Elaine and Willis on the porch, their eyes pointed in his direction. He saw Elaine say something to the stable hand, who nodded and headed after Dillon. It seemed as if visiting time was at an end.

"I think I better get back to work," Noah murmured, pulling his gloves out of his pocket and shoving his hands into them.

Matthew looked from Dillon to Noah, and frowned. "I didn't get you in trouble or anything, did I?"

Noah shook his head and tried to look as if he weren't disappointed at having to say goodbye. "No. It's okay. I just... I have a lot to do."

Matthew nodded but still looked concerned. "All right. If you're sure. Thanks for... uh... looking after The Bean. I probably won't be long."

Noah bobbed his head. "Take your time."

"Nice meeting you, Noah," Matthew said with a small wave.

Raising his hand in farewell, Noah watched Matthew walk away towards Dillon. "My pleasure," he said too quietly for Matthew to hear.

If anyone were to ask, Matthew would never have been able to explain it. His mother always dismissed his concerns by telling him he was imagining things. Maybe. But all the same, he'd never liked Elaine and her brood, particularly her son.

Dillon was only a year younger than him, so Matthew knew him pretty well, had run into him frequently at school and gone to parties where Dillon had also been invited. They even had a few friends in common. Yet Matthew had never really warmed to the guy, despite his handsome face.

Part of it, Matthew suspected, was that Dillon had always seemed a little too impressed by Matthew's father's money, which in Matthew's book was an immediate strike against him. Too many times growing up, Matthew had learned someone wanted to be his friend—or something more—simply because Matthew's house was bigger and sat on more land than any of his classmates' homes.

It hurt to think the only thing people like that believed he had going for him was his father's bank account. Matthew would be the first to admit—he'd had nothing to do with that. Most of the money had been earned long before he was born. He reaped the benefits, sure. But he wanted his friends to like him for him, not for what his family's money could buy.

Dillon wasn't as obvious as some. But as long as Matthew had known him, he had shown an interest in things like what brand of clothes Matthew wore or where Matthew's family had taken vacation over the summer.

What was worse was Dillon's habit of never making a choice without first thinking about how it would be perceived. Every move he made seemed planned, as far as Matthew could tell, every response edited.

But most troubling to Matthew was what he thought might be a mean streak in Dillon. It was subtle, but in Matthew's opinion most definitely there. Matthew didn't know if he had ever seen Dillon laugh unless it was at someone else's expense. He was never kind when he could make a joke at someone else's expense.

"Hey, man," Dillon said to Matthew now, trotting up to meet him. "Sorry I wasn't out here to greet you. Mom says come up to the house. She's got the check and a tall glass of sweet tea waiting for you."

Much as he believed Dillon's mom to have the same calculating personality as her son, Matthew was willing to go up to the house and say hi. Not only did he need to pick up the check, but a glass of sweet tea sounded pretty good right about then.

"Thanks," Matthew said, walking alongside Dillon towards the house. "I could really go for something cold."

Dillon smiled. Matthew noted it didn't reach his eyes. "Your horse being taken care of?"

Matthew nodded. "Yeah. The kid said he'd look after him."

Dillon glanced over at him. "He didn't give you any trouble, did he?"

"Who?" Matthew asked. "Noah?"

"Yeah. Did he say anything to you?"

"No," Matthew said with surprise. "He was great. Why would you even ask?"

Dillon shrugged. "Just figured I ought to check. Come on. Let's go inside and cool off."

Seeing as he hadn't finished his work the way he'd been ordered, Noah felt fortunate all Willis did when he returned to the stable was give him a slap to the back of his head and call him a lazy little shit.

Coming from Willis, that was practically the equivalent of a love tap.

Assuring the man he would complete the tasks at hand, Noah picked up his pitchfork and got back to cleaning out the stalls. Willis seemed happy to leave him to it. Once he was satisfied Noah had enough to keep him busy, the stable hand retired to his office to work on the accounts. He left the door open; but at least he wasn't looking over Noah's shoulder.

Left as alone as he ever was, Noah couldn't help but smile to himself as he loaded up his wheelbarrow. It wasn't that the chore had suddenly gotten any less disgusting. It was just that now he had something a lot more pleasant to think about while he did it. Someone.

Matthew.

What a cool name.

A cool guy too. At least Noah thought he was. Not only was he handsome as anything, but he was nice. So nice. They might have just met, but Matthew had treated Noah like a friend, like someone who mattered.

It had been a long time since anyone other than his grandmother had done that.

What would it be like to actually be friends with someone like that? Someone who was funny and kind, and who rode a horse like he was a combination of John Wayne and James Bond. He was just so...

Great. He was great.

And Noah was very, very small. If not in height, then in

importance.

Noah sighed as he moved on to the final stall. Nice as it had been meeting Matthew, it wasn't anything he should let himself dwell on. He was being stupid. He knew that. Not only was the guy years older than him, but he was going away at the end of the summer. It wasn't like they were going to be best buddies anytime soon. Noah would just have to get over his crush.

Crush?

When had he started thinking of Matthew like that?

Even considering the idea, Noah could feel himself starting to blush, which was ridiculous. No one was there to see him and there was no way anyone could know how he felt. About Matthew or anything else. Still, those feelings—new and exciting though they were—had the power to make him...embarrassed.

And hot in a way the Texas sun never had.

He still couldn't entirely believe it.

But he thought he might like boys more than he liked girls.

It was all theoretical, of course. It wasn't like he had his pick of boyfriends and girlfriends, and could compare one against the other. He might have figured out what his right hand was for. But in reality, he lived like a hermit. A hermit whose room was located directly across the hall from his grandmother. He had never been intimately touched by any hand other than his own, had never even been kissed. Yet in spite of his inexperience, Noah had begun to have an inkling which way his preferences lie.

He'd started to notice how anytime something romantic was on television, his eyes were always drawn to the male half of the couple. At first, he'd told himself he was paying attention to the guy to learn how those sorts of things were done. After all, he didn't exactly have any peers he could go to with questions about that kind of thing. And he was fourteen now; he had to figure it out somehow. But it didn't take long before he'd realized he wasn't really keeping an eye on the hero to try and be like them.

He was hanging on their every word, their every move, because he wanted to be *with* them.

And that was a lot to take in.

"I don't know, man. That's right around when I'll be heading down to UT. I'm not sure I can make it."

Matthew! His heart doing jumping-jacks inside his chest, Noah nearly dropped his pitchfork. He'd been so engrossed, he hadn't heard anyone approach.

"Check and see. Everyone from school is going to be there. I'm pretty sure your mom has already RSVPed for your family."

"She has?"

"That's what my mom said."

"Well...then I guess we're coming."

Damn it. He was with Dillon. Much as Noah would have liked to have said goodbye to Matthew, to see him one last time and wish him well at school, he wasn't sure that was such a good idea with his stepbrother around. One of Dillon's favorite hobbies was to humiliate Noah. And really—dressed as Noah was, doing the kind of work he was doing—the opportunities for that kind of thing at the moment were endless. Noah didn't want Matthew to witness that. So he stayed tucked away, silent and still, in the far corner stall.

"Well, thank your mom again for her hospitality," Noah heard Matthew say as, with Dillon, he circled around the side of the stable to collect The Bean.

"It was no trouble," Dillon said. "You're always welcome."

"Thank Noah for me too, would you. He seems like a nice kid."

Back pressed flat against the stable wall, Noah grinned. All right. At least he'd made a good impression.

"Glad you think so," Dillon said, clearly implying he didn't.

Noah could hear the creak and groan of leather. Matthew must have mounted his horse.

"Who is he, anyway?" Matthew asked.

"Noah?"

"Yeah."

Dillon chuckled. "Nobody."

Sighing, Noah closed his eyes and bowed his head. Great. It appeared it was possible for him to be humiliated without even being present.

"Don't be an ass, Dillon," Matthew said, disgust ringing in his tone. "Everybody is somebody." Noah heard nothing more said. But almost immediately the sound of hoof beats pounding against the ground reached his ears. Matthew was on his way home.

From his place inside the stable, Noah could only open his eyes and smile, his head tipped back against its resting place. Well, what do you know? It turned out he didn't have a crush on Matthew at all.

He was already halfway to falling in love.

"Mom, tell me you did not commit us to going to your friend, Elaine's, barbeque."

"Matthew, honey, did you get the check?"

"Yes, I got the check," Matthew said, digging it out of his jeans' pocket and setting it on the countertop. "Now please answer my question. Did you tell Elaine we would all attend her party?"

"Yes, I did," his mother said, coming into the kitchen, where Matthew was pouring himself a glass of lemonade. "She's my friend and she made a point of asking me in person. It's just a party. Stop making it sound like it's the end of the world."

"That's the day before I'm supposed to leave for Austin," he said, closing the refrigerator, and turning to look at her, brows pulled down into a frown.

His mother shrugged. "So? You can be packed and ready to go before it starts. We won't stay long. It's not one of those kinds of parties. From what Elaine has told me, it'll be mostly families attending. You'll probably be able to say a final goodbye to a lot of your friends."

Leaning back against the counter, Matthew sighed and took a sip of his lemonade. He supposed that could be a good thing. It would save him making a bunch of phone calls.

"Sweetheart," his mother said, walking over to him and putting a hand on his arm, "what's the big deal?"

Matthew made a face. "You know I'm not crazy about that family."

"Oh, come on," his mother said, crossing past him to pull a cutting board out of the drawer. "I've known Elaine for years. She's not that bad. I can't tell you how many times she's come through for me with the auxiliary."

"So you say," he murmured.

"So I do," she confirmed with a smile. "Now get out of here. I want to get my marinade started for tonight's dinner and you're in my way."

"Far be it from me to stand between your cooking and my appetite," Matthew said, leaning over to give her a kiss on the cheek. "If you need me, I'll be seeing if I can better my score at Madden."

"Have fun," she called after him.

Taking his lemonade with him, he headed into the family room. So, it looked like he had plans for the third Saturday in August. Much as he would have liked to have blown off the barbeque, doing so would only aggravate his mother. And he didn't want to leave town with her being angry at him. Besides, she had a point about him being able to see his friends one last time.

Still, a part of him wanted not to go simply because Dillon was so interested in seeing him attend.

What a jerk. Matthew couldn't believe how dismissive the guy had been about that kid at the stable—like just because he was shoveling shit to make some money, he had no value at all.

Noah had been nothing but nice to him, and had taken good care of The Bean. When would Dillon learn those were the kinds of things that were important, not the way a person looked or what they did for a living?

Of course, there was nothing really wrong with the way Noah looked, Matthew admitted to himself as he settled down on the couch and reached for the game controller. Matthew had no idea how old the guy was, but he was definitely at the gawky stage, on his way to tall but somehow the rest of his body hadn't quite figured it out yet. Still, he'd grow into himself. Give him a couple of years, a decent haircut, and some clothes that weren't spattered with manure, and the boy would be a looker. He already had a killer smile...

Oh great, he thought to himself. He might not know Noah's exact age, but he was pretty damn certain the kid was young. Maybe even in junior high. Which meant, with thoughts like that, Matthew was well on his way to becoming a cradle robber.

Chuckling ruefully to himself, Matthew shook his head. "Oh, man. I have got to get laid."

He debated calling Charlie to see if maybe he wanted to do something. What they had together wasn't serious, but it sure was fun. Not even Cal walking in on the two of them had dulled the attraction.

Maybe after dinner, he told himself, as his team lined up before him on the widescreen. After all, if he wanted to figure out where he stood on the whole gay thing, it was probably a good idea for him to get more experience.

~*~*~*~

When Noah had overheard Matthew and Dillon talking about the party Elaine was planning to throw, he wanted to learn more. Especially if there was a chance Matthew might attend.

"I'd heard Dillon talking to that guy who came to see you," he said, choosing his words carefully. "He said you'd invited his family to a party."

"Yes," Elaine said. "Matthew's family will be there. We've actually invited quite a few families to join us. It's the third Saturday in August. I'm having it catered. There will be fireworks and dancing too. Should be quite a crowd."

Fireworks, Noah thought, a plan forming inside his head. Perfect.

But he tried not to seem overeager. "That sounds like a lot of work. What are you going to need me to do?"

Elaine looked at him, bemused. "Nothing. You won't be attending, Noah."

"Well, no—not attending exactly," he said hurriedly. "But...if you're going to have that many people coming, won't you want—?"

"What I'll want is for you to be out of the way," Elaine said. "I expect you to be upstairs with your grandmother."

"But I—"

"I'm sure she'd be terribly lonely if she were up there all by herself. And you know it's out of the question for her to attend. That kind of excitement isn't good for someone in her delicate condition."

Noah was sure of no such thing. His grandmother might be frail, but she certainly had enough strength to sit and visit with other people. Even people besides him.

Still, he knew if he pushed any further, Elaine would realize how important the party was to him. And that wouldn't be good. Over the years, Elaine had made a habit out of taking away what Noah cared about most. He wasn't going to let her have this too.

"You're probably right," he said with a small smile and a nod. "I'd just figured you'd have something for me to do."

Elaine considered him for a moment, as if weighing his sincerity. But, in the end, she let the matter drop. "No, not this time."

It was all Noah could do to keep from sighing with relief.

The day of the party dawned sunny, yet cool for August.

"Oh, thank goodness," Elaine said, standing on the front porch and looking up at the brilliant blue sky, while Noah swept up nearby. "We've got too many people coming to have them all indoors. I was hoping the weather would cooperate. Now hurry, Noah, and get your chores done. I want you upstairs by the time the caterers get here. And remember—for no reason are you to come down. Is that understood?"

"Yes, Ma'am."

Noah had just finished up his duties at the stable when two large white panel trucks pulled up the drive. Stowing away his tools, he trotted past the workers and into the house. Dripping with sweat despite the moderate temperature, he started stripping off his dirty clothes as soon as he reached the third floor. He could hear the bustle of the caterers unloading their equipment bleeding through the door from downstairs.

"What's going on?" his grandmother asked.

"Elaine has some big barbeque planned for tonight," he said, peering into her room. She was seated in her chair with a book on her lap. "The caterers just arrived to set up."

"What are you doing?" she asked with a frown.

"I'm getting cleaned up," Noah said, flashing her his biggest smile.

She looked stunned. "You're invited?"

"Nope," he said with a shake of his head. "I'm crashing the party."

"Noah, no," she said, clearly concerned. "Elaine will get angry."

"No she won't, Grandma," he assured her, coming to kneel beside her chair. "Don't worry. I'm not going to do anything to make her upset. I just want to say hello to someone. That's all."

"Who's this?" she asked.

"Matthew," he said. "Remember, I told you about him. The guy with the pinto?"

She thought about it for a moment. Her memory kicked in slowly at times. "With the funny name?"

"Yeah," he said, grinning. "That's the one. The Bean. I love that name."

She smiled back at him, but with far less enthusiasm. Reaching out, she ran her fingertips lightly along the curve of his cheek before taking hold of his hand. "Be careful, dear," she warned. "Elaine...can't be trusted."

"I know, Grandma," Noah said, giving her hand a gentle squeeze. "Believe me, I know. But it's no big deal. I'll be in and out before she even knows I'm there."

Noah's grandmother nodded. But she didn't look convinced.

Noah waited until after Lucy had brought up dinner to put his plan in action. They were serving authentic Texas barbeque. Everything looked and smelled delicious. But he was far too excited to eat.

He was going to see Matthew again. Even if only for a moment or two.

Hurriedly, he got dressed.

By the time night had fallen and enough ticks of the clock had gone by for dinner to give way to dessert, Noah figured the moment was right for him to make his move.

"Wish me luck," he said to his grandmother, unable to control his nervous smile.

"Always," she murmured, her expression worried.

Treading lightly, Noah crept down the stairs from the third floor to the second. He knew this staircase as well as he knew anything, and he used that knowledge to avoid every creaking floorboard and to keep from tripping over any uneven tread. He made it to the second floor undetected.

"One down, one to go," he whispered to himself, wiping his damp palms on the legs of his jeans, and psyching himself up for phase two.

He'd taken particular care getting ready for that evening's excursion. Noah didn't really own any "good" clothes. What would have been the point? Still, this particular pair of jeans fitted him better than any other, and the blue and white striped shirt he wore over it didn't overwhelm him as badly as some others in his closet. He couldn't do anything about his hair or his skin. But it wasn't as if Matthew didn't already know what he looked like. And he'd seemed to like Noah well enough as he was. It would have to do.

Getting from the second floor down to the entryway and out the door was going to be the hardest part of his plan. Once he was outside, Noah figured he had a good chance of going undetected what with the dark and the crowd. But first he had to actually get out of the house, which he was certain would prove far more challenging.

Poised behind the door separating the third floor stairs from the second floor, Noah waited for his cue.

When he heard the pops and cheers of delight from outside, he knew the time had come.

Fireworks. The perfect cover.

If he'd planned correctly, everyone should be watching them

and not who was coming and going from the house.

He moved as quickly and as carefully as he could down the first flight of stairs. Once at the bottom, he peered over the landing's railing to see if anyone was walking around in the foyer below.

The coast was clear. Trembling with a mix of adrenaline and fear, he dashed down the final flight of stairs, out the front door and down the porch steps. There were no witnesses.

Freedom! Now all he had to do was find Matthew.

The guests were congregated on the side lawn, way in the back. The fireworks crew had set up on the field just beyond, so standing there afforded everyone the best view. The front porch and the walkway leading up to it were well lit. Temporary lighting had been brought in for the party, so the area from where the cars were parked to where the caterers had arranged the tables and seating was brighter than it would have been naturally.

Noah avoided all that as best he could, choosing instead to circle the long way around, keeping to the shadows, and edging carefully around the stable's solid, silent mass. He figured the building would be good protection from curious eyes. Once he got past that, he should be able to work his way unnoticed towards the party's fringe, as he would be coming up from behind.

Yet before he'd gotten halfway down the stable's longer side, he heard movement from just up ahead. In the distance, Noah could see two figures—they looked to be men—coming along the path leading from the yard to the stable. Quickly, he ducked back out of the way and out of sight.

"Charlie, where are we going?" whispered a familiar voice.

"Shh! Come on. I'll show you."

Noah flattened himself to the wall, beside the barn door there. It had been left open just a crack. His heart was pounding so violently in his chest, the reverberations from it were making him nauseous.

Oh, God. Matthew. And he was with another guy. Someone named Charlie.

"Come on, Matt. In here."

"What—the stable?" Noah heard Matthew say. "Are you crazy? Anyone could come in here!"

"For what?" Charlie replied, with what sounded like amusement. "A midnight ride? Get real. Everyone is over there watching the pretty fireworks. We've got some time."

"There is no way I can take getting interrupted again," Matthew warned, his voice coming now from inside the stable. He might be protesting, Noah thought. But Matthew was following Charlie's lead. They must have entered through the door opposite where Noah stood. "I'm telling you. I may be young. But my nerves can't take it."

"Cal isn't here tonight, is he?"

"No. He and the guys have a gig in Dallas."

"Then we should be good."

"Dude. There are other people who could walk in on us. My *parents* are here."

"Guess we'll just have to be quiet then. And quick. Come here, handsome. Let's have some fun."

It wasn't until Noah heard the faint rustle of clothing, and a muffled gasp followed by soft wet sounds that he realized just how naïve he really was. Or maybe simply how stupid. Listening to their conversation, he hadn't really gotten at first why Matthew and his friend had stolen away to the stables together. Now, listening to the soundtrack of their tryst, he understood why they'd come seeking privacy.

They were kissing. And maybe even getting ready to do more.

Noah knew it was wrong. That doing this was no different from spying and most likely illegal. But he absolutely needed to see what was going on inside.

He inched his way forward until he could peek in through the open barn door. Peering inside, he saw Willis had left on a single work lamp. Its bulb dangled from the rafter overhead, casting a perfect circle of white onto the floor below. The light faded softly beyond its boundary, casting a moody glow.

There, just outside that circle, he could make out Matthew and Charlie. Matthew's back rested against a narrow partition separating two of the stalls, Charlie was facing him, his chest pressing against Matthew's. Charlie's hands were stroking along the sides of Matthew's body. Matthew's palms were tracing the slope of Charlie's back, languid and sweet as honey. They were kissing, just like Noah had guessed they would be, mouths open and eager.

Noah slicked his lips with his tongue as he looked on, and concentrated on not making a sound. He couldn't believe he was seeing this. While he might have happily confessed to being head over heels for an oblivious Matthew, he'd never in a million years have believed the object of his infatuation also liked men. What were the odds? Yet that clearly seemed to be the case.

Noah watched as Matthew's hands slipped low to cup the curve of Charlie's ass. He squeezed the taut muscle there and released, leisurely and strong, his fingertips teasing the center seam. After a moment or two of that attention, Charlie broke off from their kiss, tucked his forehead in the space between Matthew's shoulder and jaw, and moaned, low and lost.

It was all Noah could do to keep from moaning right along with him.

"What do you want?" Charlie murmured, lifting his face so he could press a string of soft, moist kisses from Matthew's chin to his ear. Matthew tilted back his head, closed his eyes, and let him. "Tell me what you want."

"Suck me," Matthew muttered, his own hands going to the button on his fly and popping it open. But before he could lower the zipper, Charlie stopped him.

"Ah, ah, ah," he said softly. "Let me unwrap my own present."

Matthew opened his eyes and chuckled. "Hurry, then. You know we haven't got much time."

Charlie got down on his knees. It only took a moment for him to free Matthew from his jeans and boxer briefs and take hold of him, his grip tight and sure. Matthew hissed when Charlie closed his hand around him, and buried his own fingers in Charlie's thick brown hair to pull him nearer to where he wanted Charlie to be.

"Come on, man," Matthew urged, his voice rumbling out low and tattered. "Don't fucking tease."

Charlie grinned up at him and moved his hand up and down

in slow, lazy strokes. "You sure? I'm told I'm kinda good at it."

"Charlie..."

Oh Christ, Noah thought, feeling his own arousal begin to harden and stir. Matthew was practically begging for it.

"Easy," Charlie said, pressing a kiss to the vee of skin revealed by Matthew's open fly, his hand still moving. "Easy, now. I've got you."

And saying nothing more, he closed his lips around the tip of Matthew's cock before sliding down to swallow most of it.

Matthew whimpered, his hands clenching in Charlie's hair, closed his eyes and seemingly gave himself over to the wet drag and pull of the other man's mouth.

Noah couldn't catch his breath. His pulse felt like it might beat right through his skin. Sweet Lord. He'd never seen anything like it.

Charlie was a good-looking guy. Tall, well-built, with delicate, almost feminine features and expressive eyes. But he was nothing next to Matthew, who was gorgeous in everyday life, and absolutely incandescent like this. His hips rolled with Charlie's ministration, restless and needy. His lips parted on a soft wordless sound, kiss-swollen and red. And his cheeks, they flushed with a warmth—with a fire—Noah could see burning from halfway across the stable. Unbelievable. Matthew was so damned beautiful chasing pleasure. The only thing that would have been more perfect was if Noah had been the one giving it to him. Noah could have watched him forever, all strung out on want, and desperate for it.

Only it didn't seem as if Matthew would be able to hold out nearly that long.

"Charlie," Matthew whispered, his voice hoarse like he'd been screaming, or had been trying very hard not to. "Charlie... I'm gonna... I..." And with a shudder, he curled over the man at his feet, his hands clutching at Charlie's shoulders, and let go, gasping his release.

Charlie stayed with him the whole way, his mouth moving slick and tight, until finally Matthew pulled him away and to his feet. With Charlie all but burrowing now against Matthew, both guys scrabbled madly at the button fly of Charlie's jeans, fumbling it open enough for Matthew to slip his hand inside. It only took a few determined strokes on Matthew's part before he had Charlie crying out and coming apart in his arms. Afterwards, Matthew held Charlie close, his hands smoothing over him, waiting patiently while the other man calmed. When he did, it was with a sigh.

"That was fun," Matthew murmured.

Charlie pulled back to look at him, his expression fond. "That's one word for it."

Matthew chuckled.

"You gonna miss me when you're in Austin, Matt?" Charlie asked, his palms running lightly over Matthew's shoulders and arms.

"If I say yes, it'll only make you more full of yourself than you already are," Matthew said, smiling.

Charlie pouted. "Oh now, don't be mean. I'll miss you."

Matthew reached up and pushed Charlie's hair back from his forehead. "No, you won't. You'll be up in the Big Apple, breaking hearts and taking names. You're going to forget all about me."

Charlie smoothed his thumb along Matthew's cheek. "You never forget your first."

"Likewise," Matthew said, pressing a kiss to his brow.

Suddenly, both men stilled.

"Did you hear something?" Charlie asked.

Matthew was already tucking himself back into his clothes. "Fuck. I thought I heard voices."

"Me too," Charlie said, closing up his jeans. "What time is it?"

Matthew checked his watch. "After ten. I'll bet the fireworks are over."

"Which means folks will probably start heading home," Charlie said.

"Which means my parents are going to be looking for me," Matthew said with a grimace. "Let's get out of here."

Noah quickly backed away from the doorway, fearful the two might try and make their exit using a different door than the one they'd used before. He needn't have worried. Both headed out the door across from him. Pressed flat against the stable wall, Noah let loose a deep and heartfelt sigh.

Well. How about that?

He shouldn't complain. He'd gotten what he'd come out for. More or less. More, in that he'd gotten to see Matthew in a way he never would have believed possible. And less, because Matthew didn't actually get to see him back.

But maybe that's for the best, Noah thought. What would they possibly have had to talk about? If he'd actually gotten some face-time with Matthew, it would have been all small talk and niceties, neither of which Noah had much experience with. He probably would have made an ass out of himself, and that would have been the way Matthew would have remembered him. If he ever even thought of him at all in the years to come. At least that day when Matthew had come over on The Bean, he'd said Noah seemed nice.

That was something.

Better nice than nothing.

Better to have known Matthew in this way, to have seen him even for so short a time, than to never have known him at all.

Noah bowed his head and sighed. Another thing he couldn't have.

You'd think he would be used to the feeling by now.

Annoyed suddenly, with himself and the situation, he shook his head. Cut it out, he said inside his head. You're being pathetic. Quit feeling sorry for yourself and focus on getting back to the house without getting caught.

Noah looked around and considered his options. Matthew and Charlie had been right. While they'd all been preoccupied, the fireworks show had come to an end. From his place hidden in the shadows cast by the stable, Noah could see people beginning to wander away from where the festivities had been held and heading off towards their cars. To get back to the house, he would need to cut directly through that foot traffic.

Which was possible, but complicated matters.

Damn. He had left it too long. He'd allowed himself to get distracted and now his window of opportunity had slammed shut. Noah had no doubt he could cross through the crowd without arousing much suspicion. It was who he might run into once he was inside the house that was his biggest concern.

Maybe he could just spend the night out there with the horses. There had to be a way he could pretend he'd simply gotten up early and come out to get started on that day's chores. Elaine, Dillon and Lucy were bound to sleep in the next morning after all the previous evening's excitement. He could use that to his advantage.

It could work. It would have to. To do anything else was too risky.

At peace with his decision, Noah checked to see no one was looking in his direction before sliding the stable's barn door open a few inches more and slipping inside.

"Well, well, well. Look who we have here."

It had never occurred to him someone might already be there, waiting for him.

Willis ambled out of his office, looking rumpled but alert, his eyes hard, his posture tense. He must have been inside the entire time, listening to Matthew and Charlie, an audience, just like Noah had been. "You wanna tell what you're doing out here?"

Noah's brain went into lockdown mode. He couldn't think at first, couldn't even form words. What could he say? What lie could he tell? "I...uh...I wanted to see the fireworks."

Willis pretended to consider that. "See now—I can't say as I believe that." He walked over to the door through which Noah had just entered, peered outside for a moment before sliding it shut and throwing the bolt afterwards. "If a person had been standing over here, on this side of the building, like you were just now, they wouldn't have been able to see anything. Not with the stable and the trees in the way. So my guess is fireworks didn't bring you out here. I just have to ask myself what did."

"It was...nothing," Noah said, struggling to come up with something—anything—Willis might actually believe. "I-I just—"

"Was it the two queers?" Willis asked it like they were friends commiserating over a common problem. "Did you come out here for them?"

Noah felt as if someone had ripped open the top of his head and poured in ice water. The chill ran all the way through him, traveling the length of his spine. "What? No! What...what are talking about?"

"Those two pretty boys who came stumbling in here just now, disturbing my nap," Willis said, taking a step forward. "I was minding my own business, trying to get some shuteye, when they decided to get all up close and personal right here in my stable. Did you know they were gonna be here, Noah? Did they invite you to come watch?"

"No," Noah said, backing away, frightened on Matthew's behalf. He could only imagine what might happen if word got back to Matthew's parents. "That's nuts."

"Could be," Willis said, still advancing on Noah, his expression turning cunning and a little bit cruel. "But you know what's worse?"

Noah shook his head.

"If they really didn't know you were out here," Willis said. "Because then you must have been spying on 'em, like some sick fuck with his pants around his ankles and his dick in his hand."

The guilt Noah had felt before at playing voyeur welled up again, threatening now to drown him like a wave at high tide. "It wasn't like that."

"Oh no?" Willis asked, reaching out to grab hold of Noah's shirt, his fingers fisting the fabric high on Noah's chest. "What was it like then, Noah? Tell me. Did you pick up any pointers?"

Noah closed his hands around Willis' wrists and tried to wrestle free, but Willis wasn't budging. "Let go of me."

"Or what?" Willis said, leaning in so close that for one crazy second Noah thought he might actually try to kiss him. "You think you can do something about it? You want to actually try? Go ahead. I think I'd like to see that. You stupid little faggot."

All at once terrified, by the label and what Willis' use of it implied, Noah gave up all pretense at cool, trying instead to twist and pull at Willis' grip on him, desperate suddenly to get loose.

Yet even though Noah had a couple of inches on the older

man, Willis outweighed him and was a far more seasoned fighter. Hooking his ankle around the back of Noah's leg, Willis pulled him off balance, and spun him, slamming him hard against the wall, stealing the air from Noah's lungs.

"I've known you were trouble, boy, since the first time I laid eyes on you all those years back," Willis growled into Noah's face, his forearm pressed firm against Noah's windpipe, his hands locking Noah in place. "I told your stepmom, the older he gets, the harder he'll be to control."

Noah was pushing back against Willis' grasp, but his panic and the lack of oxygen were making him even more uncoordinated than usual. He couldn't seem to get the other man to move.

"And now I catch you disobeying her orders," Willis continued, his breath bathing Noah's face, something sharp and foreign in its scent. Noah wondered if it might be alcohol. "You're out here wandering around on your own, lying, hiding in the shadows, acting like some kind of pervert."

"'m not" Noah said, panting, the edges of his vision beginning to gray out.

"What next?" Willis asked him. "You gonna start stealing? Or maybe peeking in on your sister or your momma? Hell, it probably ain't safe anymore having you around decent folks. You could kill us all in our sleep."

"No," Noah gasped, clawing at him now to no effect. "You're c-crazy."

"I'd be doing everybody a favor by teaching you a lesson." Willis said it as if convincing himself it were true.

And with that, he let Noah go.

Only to draw back his fist and launch it towards Noah's jaw.

When it hit, the pain exploded in Noah's head, radiating from the point of impact in crippling waves of hurt. He cried out and crumpled to the floor, his arm curved over his head for protection.

"Gotta make sure you understand you can't just run around doing whatever you want," Willis said, hauling him back up again. "You hear me?" This time when the punch was thrown, it landed in Noah's gut, bending him nearly in half. It was all he could do not to throw up the meager contents of his stomach all over the floor and their shoes.

"There are rules to be obeyed, Noah," Willis told him before hitting him again, inches from where he'd hit him last. Noah could only groan in response. "And consequences to every action. You know what they say—don't do the crime if you can't do the time."

Then his fist connected again.

Noah tried to defend himself, to block Willis' attack and maybe even connect a time or two on his own. But his attempts lacked power and aim, and Willis was easily able to deflect them.

"You think you can take me?" Willis taunted, laughing as, with another blow, and then another, he punished his victim. "Give it up, son. You're outclassed."

Noah stayed on his feet as long as he could, using the wall at his back to help keep him upright. But when one particularly vicious jab caught him under the chin, snapping his mouth closed and his head into the wall behind him, he could stand no more. Whimpering, his knees gave out and he curled forward, twisting to land on his side, where he rested, gasping for breath, his arms wrapped loosely around his middle.

For a moment, he lay there panting, unable to move, terrified of what might happen next. Everything hurt. Everything. One eye was swollen completely shut, the other he couldn't see much out of past his tears. Noah could taste blood on the back of his tongue, and knew more of it stained his face and knuckles.

Oh God. If he lived through this, what was he going to tell his grandmother?

"Come here, you sorry piece of shit."

Noah felt but couldn't see Willis grab hold of him by the back of his shirt and drag him across the floor. Even that slight movement made his stomach roll and churn.

He would not throw up, he told himself. He wouldn't. That one thing he would not do.

Please. Please don't let him throw up.

He heard a door open. Then Willis lifted him slightly and

tossed him a distance. Landing hard in a messy tangle of limbs, Noah realized he could smell leather and silver polish close by. Lying on his side, he blinked to try and bring his vision into focus. When he did, he saw he was on the floor of the tack room.

"You're gonna spend the night in here," Willis told him, standing in the doorway, silhouetted by the light behind him. "It'll give you time to think, to consider what you did wrong tonight, and figure out a way to never, ever do it again."

He turned to leave, the doorknob in his hand, but paused and looked back at Noah over his shoulder. "I mean it, kid. Don't let me catch you messing around again. Because I promise you—if I do, tonight will seem like we were just roughhousing." With that, he closed the door and locked Noah inside.

Bringing his knees up and in close, Noah rested his cheek against the cool cement floor, hugged his arms around his chest, and closed his eyes.

He would have prayed.

Only, at this point, he was pretty sure no one was listening.

Matthew took to the University of Texas at Austin with the same ease with which he seemed to take to most things, relishing the independence gained by leaving Valley View and his loving, if somewhat overprotective, parents behind.

He went through rush his freshman year, encouraged by his father to trade in on his legacy status and pledge with one of the more prestigious frats on campus. In the end, though, wary of all the parties and the seeming expectation he'd conform to some ill-defined yet highly revered house identity, Matthew chose to stay where he was--in a rambling old frame house just west of campus.

What had been, in its day, a large family home, had been cut up into four apartments, two on each floor. Matthew shared his with an Engineering major named Trevor and a guy he'd gone to high school with, Jerome, who was undecided, like Matthew was.

Matthew hit it off with both his roommates and the other young men who called the house their home. But he didn't spend all his time at the apartment. He got involved with club sports, UT's Habitat for Humanity chapter, and took part in one of the university's peer tutoring programs.

It didn't take Cal long to scrounge up a fake ID for him. So whenever Matthew had an evening he could spare from studying, and Cal and his band were in town, the two friends were together, listening to music or having a beer at one of downtown Austin's many bars.

In April of his freshman year, Matthew announced to his parents his decided major.

"Communication Studies."

"What's to study?" his father asked, shrugging. "Seems to me you communicate just fine."

Matthew might have only been a freshman, but he had an advanced degree when it came to managing his father. "Being able to get a message across is key in business, Dad. You know that. And Communication is a major that looks good on a law school application or if I decide to go on and get my MBA."

Satisfied with what the decision might mean for his son's future, Matthew's father allowed himself to be convinced.

"Study hard, honey," Matthew's mother said, smiling, seemingly aware of her son's deft handling of the situation.

And Matthew did, not because he particularly cared about becoming a lawyer or some kind of tycoon, although he hoped one day there would be the perfect role for him within his family's business. He excelled in school because what he was learning was interesting to him. It was as simple as that. He knew the same couldn't be said of all his UT friends.

Matthew came out to his parents over Christmas break his sophomore year. They took it as well as could be expected-- stunned silence followed by fast assurances his mom and dad loved him no matter what. He believed them. But they were all very careful around each other until he went back to school. It took months before the family was able to work past that initial awkwardness.

The announcement was prompted by Matthew's first serious relationship. His boyfriend's name was Stephen Lindsey. Stephen was a senior Communication Studies major who worked part-time as a reporter for The Daily Texan, UT's student newspaper. He was slender and tall, with auburn hair, green eyes, and one of the most exuberant laughs Matthew had ever heard. Stephen drank his coffee black and strong, chewed on the end of his pen when he was thinking, and squinted at the board in class because he was too vain to wear glasses. Matthew fell for him, fast and hard, and for a while they were happy. But by the time the school year ended and Stephen had graduated, their romance was over. Matthew didn't regret it. Stephen and he had parted as friends.

His four years at UT passed quickly for Matthew, as time tends to do when a person is content with their lot. When graduation loomed on the horizon, and Matthew looked back on his time in Austin, he realized he had a single regret--that he'd never had the chance to study abroad. UT offered plenty of options, but with all his on-campus activities, friendships and responsibilities, Matthew had never been able to figure out the right time to be away, not for an entire semester.

Learning of his son's disappointment during one of their weekly phone calls, Matthew's father said, "If you want to travel, your mother and I can help you with that. In fact, if you keep doing the level of work you've been doing and graduate with honors, we'll make it your graduation present. An old-fashioned grand tour of Europe. What do you say?"

What Matthew said was he had the most generous parents in the world.

So after graduating magna cum laude, Matthew set out on his own to see Europe. Though he had the means to do otherwise, he opted to travel as so many young people do—backpack strapped round his shoulders, Eurail pass in hand. He spent the nights in youth hostels and the days meeting other student travelers and seeing the sights. He had so much fun, his summer trip stretched into fall. He didn't make it back to Texas until October, yet his parents didn't give him grief about the late return. They welcomed him with open arms. His homecoming was a joyous one.

Until Matthew's father got a look at some of his vacation photos.

~*~*~*~

"Dad, come on. You know I'm not trying to mess with you."

"Do I, Matthew? Because sometimes I can't help but think you do this sort of thing just to see if you can get a reaction from me."

Matthew exited the online photo gallery they'd been scanning through quite amicably not moments before, and closed up his laptop. "Right, because having you disapprove of me and the choices I've made in my life is just so freaking awesome."

His father sighed and looked at the floor. "You know I don't disapprove of you."

Matthew smiled, even though he didn't particularly feel like it. "Maybe. But of my choices...?"

"I won't lie to you," his father said, lifting his head to meet Matthew's gaze. "There are some I wish to God you wouldn't have made."

Matthew got to his feet and walked away from the couch and his father, covering his face with his hands before pushing his fingers through his hair. This was not how he'd hoped his first day back would go. "You know we've had this conversation before, right?"

"Yes, I do," his father said from somewhere behind him. "And believe me—I'd hoped we were over and done with it."

"How do you expect me to be over and done with my sexual orientation?" Matthew asked, turning around to face him.

"Son, keep your voice down," his father said, standing. "Nancy will hear you."

"I don't care," Matthew said, purposely upping the volume, indifferent to the idea that their cleaning woman might be listening in. "I've been out of the closet for years, Dad. I have nothing to be ashamed of."

His father waved him off. "That was college. Everyone

experiments in college."

"Actually my experimentation phase started in high school," Matthew said, taking some admittedly petty satisfaction at the shock registering on his father's face. "True, I played around a little bit more my freshman year at UT. But by the time I met Stephen, I'd pretty much figured out who I was and what I wanted. That's when I told mom and you."

His father lowered his eyes and shook his head before looking up again. This time, when he spoke, his voice was softer than before. "It's *why* you want this I just can't understand. I never have."

Hearing the genuine confusion in his father's voice, Matthew took a step towards him, thinking to gentle his approach. "For the same reason you want Mom and she wants you. Some things you don't choose, Dad. You know? Some things just are."

His father frowned, but he didn't look angry. "And this Antonio you took all those pictures of—is he someone who for you just 'is'?" He seemed resigned to the idea, if not entirely thrilled about it.

Matthew's smile widened. "He was."

His father lifted his brows, his confusion mounting. "Was what?"

Matthew took pity on him. "He was someone to hang out with when I was in Italy, and a pretty good tour guide, which is why he's in so many of my pictures. But that's all. It was just a casual thing, Dad. No big deal."

His father nodded, then narrowed his eyes. "In my day, they used to joke about sailors having a girl in every port. Is that how it was with you on this trip? Did you leave some heartbroken Tom, Dick or Antonio behind in every place you visited? Because if you did, will you at least please tell me you used protection?"

Matthew made a pained wordless sound before he spoke. "Do you really want to talk sex with your gay son?"

Turning pale at the thought, his father shook his head. "Hell, no."

"Then why don't I just promise you I know how to look out for myself and change the subject?"

"Probably not a bad idea." His father hesitated for a moment, seemingly trying to come up with a safe topic. "You want a drink? If there were ever a conversation that called for one, I'd say ours just did."

"Sure," Matthew said, thankful his father had let the matter drop. "Pour me a glass of whatever you're having."

Seemingly pleased they were no longer fighting, Matthew's father headed over to the bar tucked in the corner of the family room, and picked up a bottle of Maker's Mark, lifting it as if asking for Matthew's approval. Matthew nodded. "So now that you're done with school and your European tour, have you thought about what's next?"

Matthew came over and perched on one of the bar stools. "I should have known you wouldn't be able to wait before giving me the third degree."

"What are you talking about?" his father said, handing him a glass filled with a generous splash of bourbon. "You've been back nearly twenty-four hours. I think I've shown commendable restraint."

Matthew chuckled, then tapped his glass to his father's before taking a sip. The Maker's Mark went down warm and smooth. "I don't know. I mean...I haven't even decided where I'm going to live, let alone what I'm going to do. I need a little time to figure it all out."

"You know you can stay with your mother and me as long as you like. Get your bearings," his father said, taking a step closer to lean against the bar. "The holidays will be here before you know it. We'd love to have you around."

Matthew looked at his father and saw nothing but open affection looking back at him. His dad might make him nuts sometimes, and Matthew was certain his father would never fully embrace his sexuality. But he loved the old man to distraction, and knew the feeling was mutual. He'd missed his folks while he was away.

"I might just take you up on that," Matthew said, rolling his glass between his palms. "I've got a lot to do before I can begin to think about grad school or looking for a job. I don't even have a resume ready, and all my stuff is in boxes. Plus, I'd like to catch up with my friends too while I've got some time. It's been months since I've talked to anyone. It'd be nice to see what everybody's been up to."

"We should throw you a welcome home party," his father said before taking a drink.

Matthew shook his head. "I don't know. I'd hate for you and Mom to make a fuss simply because I'm back in town."

"Maybe we won't make it be only about you then," his father said with a shrug. "Halloween is just a couple of weeks off. We could throw a costume party. Kill two birds with one stone."

Matthew frowned. "That's not a lot of time to pull together some sort of elaborate party."

"Son, you know your mother. She could throw together something like that with twenty-four hours' notice, a roll of duct tape and a ball of twine."

Matthew grinned. "I don't know, Dad. I always think of Mom as more Martha Stewart than McGyver."

"You might be right," his father said with an answering smile. "Though when all is said and done, I don't think I'd want to go up against any of the three of them."

Matthew took a sip of his bourbon and nodded his agreement.

"So what do you say?" his father asked. "Do you want to give our friends a reason to dress up in funny clothes and drink my liquor?"

Matthew thought about it for about half a second before he spoke. "Sure, why not. Your liquor is always first rate. And besides, if Cal has taught me nothing over the years it's that a man should never miss an opportunity to humiliate his friends. Funny clothes it is."

Noah changed after the beating.

He had always been a pleasant boy, an obedient child, someone who followed the rules and respected authority. Outwardly, that remained the same. He did what he was told to do, worked hard and never complained or spoke out of turn, no matter how great the temptation might have been.

But that was only outwardly. Inwardly, he'd come to a decision.

Hope was for suckers.

He was tired of believing that if he were only patient enough, good enough, his behavior would be rewarded. Someone would realize the great injustices his grandmother and he had suffered and intercede, at long last giving them lives beyond the third floor.

As the years had passed and nothing had really changed, Noah had begun to question whether such rescue was possible. If so, where was this mysterious knight in shining armor? And why was he waiting so long to make his appearance?

Willis' brutality had been the final straw. That night, as Noah had laid there in the darkness, bloodied and bruised and so very frightened, he'd finally come face to face with a harsh and very real truth. No one was ever going to rescue them. No one knew who they were or cared whether they lived or died.

They didn't matter.

And wasn't that what Elaine had been telling him in one way or another now for years?

Anyone who could have helped, with the exception of his grandmother, had either deserted or betrayed him.

This was his life.

It was foolish to yearn for anything more.

So Noah didn't. Not any longer. He isolated himself behind a shield of indifference, thin as glass and transparent to any who knew enough to see beyond it. Yet, like a window in a house, it offered him some protection from the world. Just enough to survive.

He told himself if he didn't care, then he couldn't be hurt. It may have taken him years to learn that particular lesson. But with the beating, he quickly became an excellent student.

His grandmother saw the change, and understood its cause. She'd witnessed what Noah had looked like when he'd come back from the stable the morning after Elaine's party, and had cried over her grandson as she'd helped clean away the blood and bandage his wounds.

"It's all right, Grandma," Noah had told her, though he wouldn't meet her eyes. "I'm not sorry I went. I don't care what they do to me; I'll never be sorry."

She didn't understand why that party had been so important to Noah, why the boy he'd gone to see seemed to matter to him as much as he did. But she didn't care about the boy; she cared about her grandson.

She wanted to help Noah so desperately, but she didn't know how. She loved him as much as she ever had. But she had no magic wand, no way to simply wave her hand and make all Noah's heartache go away. She wasn't powerful enough. Not like she needed to be.

So she continued to be the one who showed the boy kindness, touching him gently and speaking soft words. And as he grew, that boy becoming a man, she urged him to go, to leave her behind. But he refused.

"Where would I go, Grandma?" Noah said. "I have no money, no education, no skills. Who would have me?"

"Someone would," she said to him, holding his hand tightly in hers. "Someone who deserves you."

Noah shook his head and turned away, disbelieving. But his grandmother still had faith.

No one with so great a capacity for love could ever ultimately be expected to go without, she thought. The universe wouldn't be that cruel.

And so she held out hope. Enough, she believed for both of them.

And she waited.

For just a little while longer.

One October day, when Noah was eighteen, Elaine told him to paint the steps leading to the porch.

"Make sure you scrape up the old paint first," she said. "Then sand the wood before you put the new paint down. I want it done right, Noah. Don't try and cut any corners."

Noah had no intention of doing that. He knew what would

happen if he turned in anything less than his best effort.

Besides, this was the sort of chore he actually enjoyed. As much as he currently enjoyed anything, that is. He would be able to concentrate and spend time on his work, shutting out the world while his attention was elsewhere. And when he was finished, he would be left with something new. Something he'd created.

He was almost looking forward to it.

He set to work early on a Saturday. The sky was clear above him, an almost turquoise blue. A gentle breeze chased what few clouds were scattered overhead, as if they were playing a celestial game of tag.

Noah expected the project would take most of the day and possibly even part of the next. It wasn't that the job was difficult, just time-consuming. Elaine and Willis had certainly assigned him far more strenuous tasks, and Noah had always been able to complete them.

Over the past few years, he'd grown as strong as he was tall. His shoulders had become broad and firm with muscle, his chest and arms well-shaped and powerful. He was taller now than Willis or Dillon, his legs lean and long.

His strength hadn't been developed at a gym, but with all that had been asked of him. Lifting and carrying everything from groceries to hay bales, pushing a rake or scrubbing a floor, chopping wood or digging a post hole. Every day had been a workout.

And it showed.

So he got started, his long dark hair dancing in the wind, losing himself in his work, forgetting all but the need to remove one thing and replace it with another.

But the time late afternoon had rolled around, and the sun had begun its descent towards the horizon, Noah was already laying down the first coat of paint, white as the clouds up above. He had been left alone for hours, not having seen a soul since lunch. So it came as a surprise when Lucy pushed open the front door and came out onto the porch barefoot, talking a mile a minute on her cell phone.

"Bree, you totally have to go," she said. "It's going to be a great party. You know it will be. What else would you be doing Halloween night—taking your little brother trick or treating? That's just sad at our age."

Noah had always had an unusual relationship with Lucy. She'd never bullied him as Dillon did or treated him as if he were property like Elaine. Instead, she mostly ignored him, acting like he was a piece of furniture or a houseplant, sometimes even refusing to acknowledge he was in the same room with her.

Back in the days when he had cared about such things, Noah had wondered at the reason for her behavior. Could she have wanted him out of the picture so badly, she had decided to simply pretend he was invisible?

Then, every so often, he would catch her stealing a glance in his direction when she'd thought he wasn't looking, and he'd recognize, if not pity, then a kind of fear in her eyes. He'd never figured out if she were frightened of him or scared of what he was, what he'd allowed himself to become. All he knew for certain was she tried very hard not to be alone with him.

Which made him surprised when she stayed on the porch after she noticed he was there too. Yet upon catching sight of him, she only hesitated a second before continuing around the side of the house, where the porch wrapped and ended, and taking a seat on the swing hanging there. Despite the distance, her voice still carried easily to where Noah was working.

"No, I don't know if Leo is going for sure. I haven't talked to him. But I assume he is," she continued. "Everyone I've talked to is. I don't know of anyone who hasn't been invited."

Noah hummed quietly to himself as he applied the paint in long, even strokes, trying not to eavesdrop. Yet the soft sound wasn't enough to drown out Lucy's conversation.

"I'm telling you—it's not just a Halloween party," Lucy said. "Their son—the one that graduated college this year—just got back from Europe, so this is welcome home party for him too. From what I hear, they're pulling out all the stops. And trust me, with the money that family has, all the stops should equal one damn fine party."

If he laid down the first coat by dinner, everything would

have time to dry overnight and then he could finish up tomorrow morning, Noah thought, blotting away some of the sweat beneath his bangs with the back of his hand.

"You don't have to know their son to go. It's not like it's his birthday or something. Besides, I'm almost sure you met him at Deb's Christmas party last year. You remember—the guy that got up and sang that James Taylor song with the band. Real cute, kind of tousled, sandy-colored hair? Yeah...him. Matthew. Right, from Valley View. That's where the party is going to be."

Hearing Matthew's name, Noah caught his breath and dropped his brush directly on the step he'd been painting, ruining his work and spraying drops of white across the sidewalk like a sprinkler.

"I know, I know. He's gorgeous. But don't get your hopes up. He plays for the other team. I'm totally serious. Dillon told me. I think he's got the hots for the guy. He's even coming in from school just so he can go to this thing."

Matthew. Matthew was back, Noah thought, tingling hot then cold, as if electricity were flowing through his veins instead of blood. He was living only moments away, so near...and yet so far from where Noah was.

And suddenly, softly, like a pebble pinging against a pane of glass, his shield chipped and cracked, the fault inching slowly along its surface, spidering as it traveled.

"So have I convinced you? Are you going? Yay! Now all we have to do is figure out our costumes. I hope there's something good left to rent..."

At that point, Noah lost track of Lucy's conversation, his mind instead reviewing what he already knew.

Matthew was home, finished with school and with traveling. At least for now. His family was celebrating by throwing him a costume party on Halloween. A party with an enormous guest list.

Oh God, he wanted to go. He didn't care about the party itself, lavish though he was sure it would be. But to have the chance to see Matthew again, to really talk to him this time, man to man, knowing that's what Matthew preferred...

And just like that, the window Noah had kept between him

and the world shattered.

Noah hoped again, and remembered what it felt like to dream.

He was back in the world.

Now all he needed was a little help to make his dream come true.

That night, Noah shared with his grandmother what he'd learned that day from Lucy.

"You've told me before to go, Grandma. To try and get away from here. And I've always said no," Noah said, sitting on the ottoman at her feet. "But this time...this time I have someplace I actually want to go to, someone I want to be with. Even if it's only for a few hours. I know there are risks. But I think I'm ready to take them. Will you help me?"

His grandmother laid her hand on his. "Of course I will. I'll do whatever I can."

"Thank you."

She smiled and gave his hand a squeeze. "Now tell me more about this boy."

Noah glanced down and scraped his nail over a small bit of paint he noticed dotting his jeans. "His name is Matthew, Grandma. But I don't think he's a boy anymore."

"You like him, though," she said. "You liked him well enough all those years ago to risk angering your stepmother. Why is that?"

Noah shrugged before meeting her eyes. "He was nice to me when he didn't have to be, and stood up to Dillon on my behalf."

"He sounds honorable," his grandmother said. "What does he look like?"

"Well, I haven't seen him in four years," Noah said with an embarrassed smile. "So he might have changed. But before, when he came here that summer, he was handsome. Very handsome. And tall, though not as tall as me. His hair was brown, but lighter than mine, and shorter. Kind of spiky, like he took time with it in the morning. And he has blue eyes, Grandma. Really blue—like the sky after it rains and everything is washed clean. And they're kind, you know. But it's like he sees. He notices things and he isn't afraid to tell the truth."

His grandmother looked at him for a moment, studying his expression, before asking softly, "Noah, do you consider this boy your friend?"

Noah laughed and looked away. He could feel color rising to the surface of his cheeks. "I hardly know him."

"But would you like him to be your friend?"

"Very much," he confessed after a second or two, still avoiding her eyes.

"And more?" his grandmother asked, dogged in a way she wasn't usually.

That drew Noah's gaze to her. "I don't... What do you...? Grandma, I can't..."

"Do you love him, sweetheart?" his grandmother asked, no censure in her voice. "Have you loved him all this time?"

"Yes," he whispered, before closing his eyes and shaking his head. "It's ridiculous, I know. Hopeless, like everything else. He doesn't even know I exist."

"Well then, we must get him to notice you."

Noah opened his eyes and, realizing his grandmother was struggling to rise, stood to help her. "Wait. Where are you going?" he asked.

"Come with me."

Noah trailed behind his grandmother as, using her walker, she made her way slowly to the storage room across the hall. "What are you doing?" he asked.

"I want to show you something."

Once they were inside and had turned on the light, his grandmother came to a stop in front of a large trunk, buried beneath a collection of boxes. "Can you open this for me?"

In all the time they'd lived in the house, Noah had never noticed this particular piece of luggage. It took him a few moments to unearth it. When it was free, and he'd flipped open the catch, he was surprised by what he saw.

"This belonged to your grandfather," his grandmother said. "He was a Navy pilot in World War II."

Inside, was a khaki green uniform, made of wool and trimmed in black. Its jacket was long and fitted at the waist. There was a row of medals over the breast and a notched lapel. Stored alongside it was a pair of matching pants, shirt, tie, hat, and shoes. Everything looked to be in perfect condition.

"I've held on to it all these years for sentimental reasons," his grandmother said. "Or at least, that's what I'd told myself. But maybe I had a feeling it would be needed one day. Try it on."

Noah had been examining everything with a kind of reverence. He looked up now, befuddled. "What? Why?"

"This is a Halloween party you want to go to," she said, seemingly amused by his reaction. "You'll need a costume."

"But I couldn't..."

"Of course you can. Your grandfather was tall, like you. I think it may fit. Why don't you see?"

Hesitating only a second more, Noah nodded and scooped up the uniform to take it into his room.

As his grandmother had predicted, the clothes fit him well, the jacket hugging his shoulders and nipping his waist—even the pants were long enough.

"Look at you," his grandmother murmured as he modeled the outfit, smiling wider than Noah had seen in years. "You're the spitting image. So dashing. Put on the hat. Let me see you."

Noah pushed his bangs off his forehead and slipped on the cap with its gold band and emblem. Peering in the bathroom mirror, he thought to himself his hair should really be shorter than it was to complement the uniform.

As if reading his mind, his grandmother said, "We'll trim it before the party, so you look the part."

"This is wonderful, Grandma," Noah said, grinning, before taking her in his arms. "Thank you. Thank you so much."

"Don't thank me yet," she said. "There's one more thing you'll need."

It took them nearly a half hour and a dozen boxes before Noah was able to find what his grandmother was referring to. When he discovered it, he looked over at her, his eyes wide with surprise. "It has feathers." It did, long and brightly colored ones. Sequins, trim and more made it sparkle.

"It's a Mardi Gras mask," his grandmother said, taking it from him. "I've had it for years. It's a little showy now. But I can fix that. I'll have it ready for you on Halloween."

Noah looked up from where he knelt on the floor of the storage room, his head spinning at how quickly his fortunes had changed. "That's only a week away."

"It may only be a week from now," she said, reaching out to cup his cheek in her palm, her expression fond. "But it's been years since you saw your Matthew. I'd say you've been patient long enough. Now let's get this cleaned up, and go back and sit down. I have an idea about how you can get to this party that I want to talk to you about."

~*~*~*~

"A cowboy, Cal? Really? That's the best you could come up with?"

"Playing to my strengths, man. I know what my audience wants." Cal looked Matthew over from head to toe before arching his brow. "What are you supposed to be? Fonzie?"

Matthew glanced down at his jeans, white T-shirt, leather jacket and motorcycle boots. "Hey, it's better than wearing something with tights."

"Yeah," Cal agreed with a nod. "Suppose so. You don't really have the legs to pull something like that off."

"Fuck you," Matthew said, laughing, bumping Cal's shoulder with his own as they made their way through the foyer and into the heart of the party. "At least mine are longer than yours."

"Just for that, you owe me a drink," Cal said, leaning in to be heard over the music pulsing from the corner speakers.

"You're a cheap date. It's an open bar."

The two friends wound their way through the crowd packing the first floor of Matthew's parents' home. Everything had been opened up to partygoers with the exception of Matthew's father's office. Yet even with that much generous square footage available, space was at a premium. Very few people had declined their invitation.

"Your mom pulled this all together on her own?" Cal asked while Matthew grabbed a couple of Coronas from the bartender and handed one to his friend.

Matthew took a sip and surveyed the cobwebs and candles and ghoulish jack-o-lanterns. The zombie wait-staff circulating with trays of canapés and electric green mystery cocktails. The dance floor set up in the middle of the two-storied living room, rendered fragmented and glittering by the mirror ball hanging high overhead. The additional theatrical lights mounted on poles throughout the house, gelled to cast garish pools of red and orange that suggested hellfire, and created dramatic shadows. His parents' home looked like a disco as imagined by Dante. Matthew loved it in all its campy glory. But it certainly didn't reflect his mother's sense of style.

"No," he said. "She had help. She called in a few favors and had this guy flown in from Miami. It's a little over the top. But it's kind of fun."

"You have searchlights set up on your front drive," Cal said. "I half expected to see the silhouette of a bat shining up in the sky. Trust me when I say—it's a big over the top. As far as I can tell, your Miami party planner doesn't know the meaning of the word 'subtle'."

"Hey, now," Matthew said with a smile. "Those are my people. Be nice."

"The day your people become the crowd clubbing at South Beach is the day I stage an intervention," Cal said before taking a swig of his beer.

"Speaking of which," Matthew said, leaning against the doorway leading into the dining room, "you wouldn't believe my father's latest bright idea."

"What's dear old dad up to this time?" Cal asked.

"I found out from my mom—he apparently had his assistant do a little research," Matthew said, still smarting over what he'd learned. "She compiled a list of my friends from high school—female friends—who are still single, and reached out to them personally on behalf of the family to invite them to the party. He even flew in Mia and Abby from New York on the company jet, just so they could make it. I think he's trying on the role of matchmaker for size."

"Correct me if I'm wrong, but—he knows about the whole gay thing, right?"

"Oh, yeah," Matthew said with a wry smile, amused by his father's machinations in spite of himself. "He knows. I guess it's just a case of hope springing eternal. I should probably be more annoyed by it than I am. But I figure, ultimately, it's pretty harmless. Besides, I like the idea of seeing some old friends again. I just hope no one comes here under false pretenses."

"Here's your chance to find out," Cal said, gesturing towards the entrance opposite where they stood. Framed there were two of Matthew's former classmates—one a tall, lanky blonde named Mia, and the other a short, curvy brunette named Abby—both of them beautiful as ever.

"Speak of the devil," Matthew murmured.

"Matthew!" Abby called, giving him a little wave. She was dressed as a cheerleader, not much of a stretch in terms of creativity, seeing as she had been one in high school. Still, the uniform fit as well as it ever had, and she looked awfully cute in it. Mia had come as something out of a Fitzgerald novel, her hair curled in a Marcel wave, her slender figure covered by a fire engine red sheath, dripping with fringe.

Matthew waved and grinned. Smiling, the girls headed over. Mia's flapper costume shimmered like sunlit water as they made their way through the crowd.

"You're both looking gorgeous," Matthew said, kissing each girl on the cheek and giving them both a hug. "The Big Apple must agree with you."

"More with Abby than it does with me," Mia replied. "Would you believe she's already booked her first job?"

"Get out," Matthew said. "Doing what?"

Abby grinned. "It's a music video."

"A rap music video," Mia said.

"I get to be a ho," Abby said, with more enthusiasm than the statement probably warranted. "A dancing ho."

"A sweet young thing like you?" Cal said. "That seems like quite a stretch when it comes to casting."

Matthew recalled his manners. "You guys remember Cal, don't you? Cal—Mia and Abby. They've left Texas behind to make it big in show biz."

"Show biz won't know what hit it," Cal said, playing the gallant.

Mia made a face. "The only problem is before I can do my part to knock show biz on its ass, I need to actually be working."

"You're working," Abby said.

"As a temp at a law office," Mia said, rolling her eyes. "I was thinking more in terms of actual acting."

"I realize this isn't exactly my field," Matthew said. "But isn't there supposed to be a little something called paying your dues?"

"Highly overrated," Mia said. "Overnight success is the way to go. Am I right, Cal?"

"How the hell should I know?" Cal replied. "Success and I aren't even in the same zip code."

"That's not what I heard," Abby said. "Your band-mate, Jerry, is friends with my brother Mark. And he said Jerry had told him you guys were going to Nashville soon to work with a producer there. He said this could be your big break."

Cal smiled his very best lady killer smile and said, "Well aren't you just a fella's favorite fan."

Abby blushed, her eyes shining with excitement. "I've heard your band play. More than once. I think you guys are awesome."

"I think I'm in love," Cal said, taking a step closer to Abby.

Shaking her head at the would-be lovebirds, Mia said, "So what's a girl gotta do to get a drink around here?"

Before Matthew could answer, Cal came to the rescue. "Just ask, darlin'. All you have to do is ask. What'll you ladies have?"

"I'll have what you're having," Abby said, looking up at Cal through her lashes.

"Chardonnay if they've got it," Mia said. "Otherwise whatever white wine they're pouring."

"I'm good," Matthew said, just to be a smart ass. "But thanks for asking."

Cal flipped him off before saying, "Hold tight, y'all. I'll be right back."

As they watched Cal forge a path towards the bar, Matthew said, "It's nice to see you both."

Mia smiled. "Good to see you too. How was Europe?"

"Great," Matthew said. "It was great."

"I'll bet it was hard to come home," Abby said.

"A little, I guess," Matthew said. "But I was gone a long time, almost five months. Towards the end, I started to get kind of homesick."

"Yeah," Abby said. "It's hard being away from family, isn't it?"

"I didn't think I'd get the chance to see my folks before the holidays," Mia said. "Not with what airfare costs these days. But this is fantastic. We're making a long weekend out of it. Your dad's offer came out of left field, but it's really appreciated. I've got to make sure and track him down before the evening is over to thank him."

Matthew looked away. "Yeah. About that offer..."

"Matthew, don't worry about it," Mia said. "We know he was only trying to be nice."

"I wish that was all he was trying to do," Matthew murmured before taking a sip of his beer.

"Oh, come on," Abby said, linking her arm around his. "He can't be worried his handsome son doesn't have any friends."

"It's more the kind of friends he's worried about," Matthew said, "than the quantity."

"He thinks I'm a bad influence," Cal said, returning just in time to hear Matthew's comment, but not the context surrounding it. Smiling at the girls, he handed them their drinks.

"Are you kidding?" Matthew asked. "He thinks you're a great influence. He'd probably put you in the will if you could somehow inspire me to be more like you."

"I can be very inspirational," Cal assured him.

"Oh, wait a minute," Mia said. "This isn't about you and...guys like Charlie, is it?"

Matthew nearly dropped his beer. "What do you know about

Charlie and me?"

The girls exchanged a look before Mia said, "Well you know he's still in New York, doing that advertising internship. Right?"

Matthew nodded. Charlie and he exchanged the occasional email, so he was in the loop.

"We meet up sometimes," Abby said. "Do happy hour or whatever."

"He might have mentioned you two used to be...together," Mia said as if choosing her words carefully.

"Oh, God," Matthew said with a sigh. "Please tell me he spared you guys the gory details."

"Please feel free to spare me those as well," Cal muttered, taking a sip of his beer. "I'm more delicate than I look."

"Don't worry," Mia said. "Charlie may talk some. But really, he was quite...the gentleman when it came to you."

"Hear that, Matt?" Cal teased. "Sounds like your boy is more careful with your reputation than you are."

Matthew glared, mostly in fun. "Have I mentioned today that I really don't like you? 'Cause I don't. And he is not my boy."

"Not now?" Cal asked far too innocently.

"Not ever," Matthew said, glaring even harder. "We were just kids, fooling around. I haven't even seen him in months."

Mia patted his arm. "For what it's worth, that's Charlie's take on things too."

"So are you seeing anyone now?" Abby asked.

"No," Cal said, answering for him. "Which is why his father invited you girls."

"Oh, Matthew," Mia said, trying very hard not to laugh. "I'm so sorry."

"Yeah?" Matthew groused. "Well, that makes two of us."

"Don't worry," Cal said. "When absolutely nothing happens between you, Matthew's daddy will blame him, not you two."

"Thanks for the reassurance, Cal," Matthew said. "That makes me feel so much better."

Mia shrugged. "Just because something doesn't happen between us, doesn't mean nothing will happen at all. You've got a house full of people here, Matt. You should mingle. You never know who you might meet."

Matthew pretended to be scandalized. "What? And neglect my friends?"

"Oh, don't worry about Mia and Abby, here," Cal said, putting his arms around the shoulders of both women. "I'll make sure they're well taken care of."

Mia turned her head and looked at Cal. In her heels she was taller than him. "You think you're man enough for both of us, stud?"

"I think I'm man enough to try," Cal said, smiling sweetly, unfazed by the challenge in her eyes.

Abby giggled. "This could be fun."

Matthew chuckled. "All right, all right. Everybody keep their clothes on. You've convinced me. I'll leave you three to...whatever it is you're gonna wind up doing, and say hello to our guests. Promise me you'll stay out of trouble."

"How about if I promise we won't get caught," Cal said.

Matthew pretended to think about it for a second. "Yeah. That'll work too."

~*~*~*~

When Noah's grandmother had told him her thoughts on how he could travel to Matthew's party, Noah almost gave up on the entire scheme then and there.

"Grandma, no. I'd be dead before I got there."

"Nonsense," she said. "You'll be fine."

"I've never ridden a horse before. You know that."

"You've loved and cared for Midnight since he was just a colt. He's yours, no matter what Elaine says. Trust him to keep you safe."

Oh, Noah wanted to. Really he did. But to ride the horse he'd been forbidden from even mounting, to ride any horse at all for the first time—on top of everything else, it was almost too daring to contemplate.

"Noah, what choice do you have?" his grandmother had said when he still hesitated. "Even if you could somehow get keys to one of the cars, you don't know how to drive. And you can't walk. It would take too long. You're not going to have that much time as it is. You'll need to leave for the party after Elaine and the children, and return before them."

Noah had nodded, considering what she'd said. His grandmother was right. As dangerous as it might be, he couldn't think of any other solution. Besides—even though he was anxious about the plan, part of him really wanted to take the risk. "All right. I'll do it."

The only other thing Noah had to worry about was Willis.

"Usually when Elaine asks him to guard the house, he spends the evening in the den, watching television," Noah had told his grandmother. "But if I'm careful, I should be able to make it outside without him noticing. After all, the den is in the back of the house and the TV should mask any noise."

"Just be as quiet as you can, Noah," his grandmother had urged. "And fast."

"I will. I promise."

The night of the party, Noah was nervous, but ready. "My costume is in the stable," he told his grandmother. "I smuggled it out piece by piece and hid it where Willis won't think to look. I figured it would be better to get dressed out there rather than in the house, safer. That way, if I do get stopped by Willis, he won't immediately realize what I'm up to."

"That's smart," his grandmother said. "There's only one thing you've forgotten."

Noah frowned. "What's that?"

"This," she said, handing him a black mask, which had set within its molded shape little circlets that reflected light. It was outlined by a narrow piece of gold trim. Two lengths of ribbon were attached in back to hold the mask in place.

Noah studied it. "Did you make this from that old Mardi Gras mask?"

His grandmother nodded. "Yes, I took off the feathers and most of the sequins. This is what was left."

"It's perfect, Grandma. Thank you," he said, slipping it into the front pocket of his jeans.

"May it bring you luck."

Together, they listened for Elaine and the children to leave, then waited for an additional hour.

Finally, it was time.

Noah took his grandmother's hand and said softly, "I have to go."

She stretched up to kiss him on the cheek. "Be careful."

"I will."

"I'll wait up for you," she said. "I want to hear all about your Matthew."

Noah smiled. "I'll try not to be too late."

"No," she agreed. "You must not be. Remember, you need to get Midnight back in his stall and you upstairs before everyone returns home."

"I'll remember."

With that, Noah kissed his grandmother goodbye and started down the stairs. He moved as swiftly and silently as he had the night of Elaine's barbeque all those years ago, careful to avoid making any move that might give him away.

As before, he reached the first floor undetected. Standing at the base of the stairs, Noah could hear the television in the den, the volume loud enough that it carried from the back of the house. It sounded as if Willis might be watching a war movie. Its soundtrack was loud and full of explosions. Smiling to himself at the stroke of luck, Noah made his escape through the front door.

It was a chilly night with a star spangled sky overhead and light wind. Not wanting to take any chances, Noah quickly crossed the distance between the house and the stable, keeping to the shadows as much as possible.

When he reached the horses, he was pleased to see Willis had left a light on. Just to be safe, Noah checked the office. It was empty. This time it appeared he was truly alone.

"All right," he murmured, taking a moment to summon his courage, his palms moist, his mouth dry. "Guess it's time to get this show on the road."

Stomach fluttering like a flock of frantic canaries was trapped inside, he collected the tack he needed and took it over to Midnight's stall. The stallion was inside, waiting for him, gazing at Noah calmly, his ears pricked forward in greeting.

"Hiya, boy," Noah said quietly, opening the stall and slipping inside. "How you doing tonight? Hey, listen—I need your help with something. Okay?" He lowered everything to the ground and stood, holding just a saddle pad.

"I know you've been ridden plenty of times," Noah said, placing the pad in the middle of Midnight's back. Normally he would have groomed the horse first. But with time being limited, he'd actually brushed Midnight down before he'd left the stable that afternoon. It would have to do. "You know every path on this property and you know what to do when you've got someone on your back."

Moving quickly but smoothly, Noah began putting the saddle on. He may not have actually ridden before, but he'd prepared the horses to go out countless times. He was very familiar with the process. "I've never ridden before. I think you know that. So I really don't have a clue what I'm doing. I need you to behave yourself. All right? I need you to be a friend."

If Midnight found it strange being saddled in the middle of the night, he gave no sign. He simply stood there patiently and allowed Noah to get him ready.

"Just...don't take advantage of the new guy. Please. Get me to Matthew's place and back in one piece. That's all I ask. Do you think you can do that for me?"

Noah wasn't really expecting an answer. And he didn't get one. But as he eased the bridle into place on Midnight's head, the horse nudged Noah's shoulder with his muzzle, once, then again.

Smiling, Noah pressed his palm to Midnight's cheek. "Good boy."

Working swiftly, it wasn't long before Noah had the horse ready to go.

"Okay. Just hang out for a few minutes," Noah said, patting Midnight on his flank. "I need to get dressed and then we can get out of here."

Collecting the pieces of his costume, Noah hurriedly put them on, and when he was done, hid the jeans and shirt he'd been wearing in the tack room. His mask was in his jacket pocket. He tucked his hat under his arm.

"All right, boy. Time to go."

Taking Midnight's reins, Noah led him out of the stable, using the door on the far side of the building, out of view of the house. He'd decided it would be best to walk the horse until they got some ways out. He didn't trust his ability to mount smoothly and easily on his first attempt, and wanted to have a little distance between him and Willis before he tried it.

Midnight followed along well, not making a sound beyond the dull thump of his hooves against the ground. The wind rustled the grasses and shrubs, making a shivering, silvery sound like water rushing over rocks.

When Noah felt they'd traveled far enough, he stopped, put on his hat and took hold of Midnight's bridle, looking the horse in the eye. "Please," he said quietly, smoothing his palm down the slope of Midnight's nose, just as he had the first time they'd met. "Please, boy. Be good for me."

Midnight gave no indication he understood. Yet he stood very still.

Taking a deep breath, Noah came around to the horse's left side, put his foot in the stirrup and climbed on board. Midnight took one small step back, as if trying to regain his balance. But otherwise, he remained firm.

In the saddle for the first time, Noah wanted to laugh, to holler, to give a kick and let Midnight run till daybreak. But he knew he needed to be a little more cautious than that.

"Matthew had said his folks lived two properties to the west," Noah said to himself and the stallion he was sitting on. "West is this way." He guided Midnight's head to the left. "So let's ride in that direction and see what we can find." With that, he nudged his heels against his horse's sides. Midnight obliged by taking off at an easy trot.

Yet even that gentle stride took some getting used to on Noah's part. For one thing, his hat was bouncing all over his head, which meant Noah had one hand on it and one hand on the reins, which felt a little like he was trying to pat his head and rub his stomach at the same time.

"Whoa, boy. Hold on."

When Midnight came to a stop, Noah unbuttoned his uniform jacket to the waist, pulled off his hat and shoved it inside. Buttoning the coat up over it, he knew that while he might look ridiculous, at least he wouldn't lose his hat before he'd reached the party.

"Okay, then. Let's go."

It didn't take much persuasion for Midnight to start moving again; it took even less for him to go from a trot to a canter. Once he got over his surprise, Noah whole-heartedly approved. Not only were they covering ground far more quickly, but the ride was a heck of a lot smoother. Midnight's gait was fluid and he was handling like a dream, sensitive to Noah's every movement and direction.

"Thank you, Midnight," Noah murmured fervently under his breath. "Thank you so much."

With the night being clear, Noah's eyes adjusted fairly well. He could see where paths had been created through the fields and could make out dips and crests of the hills. Yet he couldn't see any kind of buildings or signposts suggesting someone's home might lie ahead.

Then, Midnight and he came up over a rise, and Noah noticed something peculiar. Off in the distance, just past the tree line, there seemed to be an odd sort of glow. It wasn't golden like fire, but instead white like lamplight.

"That's not natural," he said to himself, wondering at the cause. "That's got to be manmade. It's westward from here. So it could be coming from Matthew's home. And even if it isn't, maybe someone there can tell me how to get to his place."

His decision made, Noah pointed his horse in the direction of the faraway glow and headed towards it as fast as he could.

~*~*~*~

It wasn't really a bad party.

Yet even so, Matthew couldn't help but feel disappointed by it.

What else could he feel when everyone seemed to be hooking up but him?

Once he'd left Cal and the girls, Matthew had wandered around as they'd urged, visiting with old friends and neighbors, and meeting new ones. Everyone had assured him what a wonderful time they were having. Booze flowed freely. The music seemed to have magical properties that urged bodies, young and old, into motion. Inviting shadows were everywhere, perfect for sneaking away to steal a kiss or maybe more, and many couples looked to be taking advantage. All in all, the stage was set.

Only Matthew couldn't find a costar.

And that was so unfair.

It might have been a Halloween party. But he was supposed to be the guest of honor.

Maybe it was the Coronas talking, but that old Leslie Gore song was beginning to echo inside his head.

By the time Dillon had cornered him in the library, dressed as a vampire and flirting as if he believed Matthew might actually be that desperate, Matthew was about to write off the evening entirely and go shoot a solitary game of pool in the billiards room.

Making the excuse of filial duty, he got away from Dillon, intent on making good his escape, when he saw someone he hadn't noticed before standing in the living room doorway.

He was tall. Really tall. Matthew was six feet, and he'd bet this guy had a couple of inches on him. He was dressed as a member of the military. Matthew thought the uniform might be genuine, rather than a costume. It looked like something from one of the world wars, olive green in color with black trim, and hugged the person wearing it as if envious of his skin. Matthew could understand the impulse.

The guy was hot.

His mystery man had wide shoulders, legs that looked as if they might be part stilts, a trim waist and a high, rounded ass. His hair was long and dark, worn pushed away from his face and held back by a hat that went with the outfit. From where he stood, Matthew really couldn't see much of the man's features, which was a shame. In addition to his hat, which rested mid-brow, the newcomer wore a mask over his eyes. Only a small number of guests had opted to go that extra step. Matthew wondered why he seemed so determined to conceal his identity. From what Matthew could tell, there wasn't any reason for the man to be shy.

Determined not to let this one get away—at least not until he'd learned if there might be a spark between them—Matthew worked his way towards him, winding through the throng of guests. The man didn't seem to sense his approach. He stood framed in the archway, scanning the crowd as if searching for someone. When their eyes finally met, it appeared he'd found what he was looking for. He froze, his mouth falling open. It seemed to Matthew he might even be holding his breath.

Surprised, Matthew couldn't figure out what might have caused such a reaction. It was almost as if the man were frightened of him.

"Hi," Matthew said when he came to stand before him. He was younger than Matthew had thought he was at first, but maybe even better looking up close. The man smelled of the outdoors rather than of cologne, of crisp fall air and clean male sweat. "I don't think we've met."

The man gazed at him a moment longer, saying nothing, before dropping his eyes and clearing his throat. "I...um...no, I guess we haven't."

"I'm Matthew," Matthew said, extending his hand. "I'm the, uh...well, my family actually—we're the hosts."

The man looked down at Matthew's hand for a second before taking it in his. His palm was warm and a little damp, but his grip was strong. "Nice to meet you. I'm N...Noel—I'm Noel."

"Hi, Noel," Matthew said, giving his new acquaintance what he knew to be his most winning smile. "Glad you could make it. Can I offer you something to drink?"

Noel hesitated yet again before nodding. "Yeah, that would be great."

"Well, come on then," Matthew said, holding out his hand before him as if pointing the way. "Let me show you to the bar.

It's a little easy to get lost in this place, especially on a night like this."

"I can imagine. You've got a great house."

"Thanks," Matthew said. "I haven't really lived here the past few years. I've been down in Austin for school. But I like it. It's still home."

Together they made their way into the dining room, which was the location of the closest bar. Once there, Matthew turned to his companion and asked, "What'll you have?"

Noel looked at the array of bottles lined up behind the bartender, squinting as if trying to read the writing on each. "Could I...um...could I get a glass of water?"

Matthew chuckled, thinking at first he had to be joking. "Water? I'm pretty sure we can do better than that."

Noel turned his way and frowned, appearing flustered or maybe simply confused. "It's just... I didn't want to..."

Oh, God, Matthew thought. Maybe there was a reason the guy was drinking water. Like he was someone's designated driver. Or he had an alcohol problem.

Great.

"Hey, man. I'm sorry," Matthew said, wanting to as quickly and as painlessly as possible extract his foot from his mouth. "I'm not trying to pressure you or anything."

"Oh, no," Noel assured him. "You're not pressuring me."

"I just thought you might like—"

"It's okay—"

"If you want water, we can get you water."

"No. Actually...what are you having?"

"Me?" Matthew said, easing up on his concern. Noel didn't seem to have taken any offense. Maybe Matthew hadn't inadvertently coaxed him off the wagon after all. "I've been drinking Coronas."

"Okay," Noel said. "I'll have one of those."

Matthew smiled at him before turning to the bartender. "Make it two."

After they had their beers in hand, Matthew tapped his against Noel's. "Happy Halloween."

"Happy Halloween," Noel echoed and took a sip, as Matthew

did. Almost immediately, he made a face, his nose wrinkling.

"Is it warm?" Matthew asked. His bottle was ice cold. But he knew it could be tricky keeping things chilled at big parties like this. Maybe the bar staff had just restocked.

Noel shook his head, then opened and closed his mouth a few times as if trying to identify a certain flavor on his tongue. "No, no. Just...different."

"Than what?" Matthew asked in surprise.

"Than...nothing," Noel said, determinedly taking another sip. "It's fine. Really. It's good."

"Good," Matthew said, confused by their conversation, but willing to let it go. "Glad you like it." Noel smiled. They each looked at each other for a moment saying nothing. Then Matthew asked, "Hey, do you want the fifty cent tour?"

Noel looked surprised yet pleased by the offer. "Sure."

"Come on."

Matthew put his hand on Noel's back as he led him through the crowd. "You've already seen the living room and dining room. That door over there to the right is the library, and to the left there is a hallway that leads to one of the guest suites."

They made their way around the edge of the dance floor, past the deejay's booth and towards the back of the house. "This is our kitchen and the breakfast room and beyond that, down the steps, is the family room."

Together, they walked over to the wall of windows looking out over the expansive back courtyard, and peered through the panes into the darkness beyond. As it was chilly, not many people were outside, save for a few diehard smokers. Matthew could see through the patio doors the fiery ends of their cigarettes, glowing like lightening bugs in the night.

"My dad's office is in the back here next to the gym and billiards room," he said, resuming the tour by leading them through the family room and out the door on the opposite wall. "Upstairs is mostly bedrooms, along with the media room and my mom's office."

"This place is huge," Noel said, seemingly not even trying to disguise his awe. "I can see what you mean about getting lost."

"It kind of is," Matthew admitted, feeling sheepish when faced with Noel's reaction. Most people tried to play it cool when they came to his parents' place, like all the Texas style size and glamour was expected. Noel didn't seem to be wired that way; his response was too honest. "My dad helped design the layout when my mom and he had first gotten married. I know they'd planned to have a big family. So I guess he'd wanted to make sure they'd have enough room. But in the end, all they got was me."

Walking down the hallway together, their shoulders glancing off each other, Noel looked over at Matthew from beneath his lashes and smiled, a pair of dimples carving dents in his cheeks. "That doesn't seem like such a bad thing."

Matthew smiled back at him, pleased.

Oh, yeah. Definite sparkage.

"Hey," Matthew said, an idea forming. "Do you play pool?"

Noel shook his head, looking vaguely embarrassed. "I'm sorry, no. I'm afraid not. But I'm willing to learn."

"Come on then," Matthew said, continuing down the corridor leading to what his mother had always jokingly referred to as his father's domain. "Let's play a couple games. If you're interested, that is. I could kind of use a break from all the noise and the crowds."

"Sure. That would be great."

The billiards room was tucked away at the very end of the hall, next door to Matthew's father's office. While it was technically open to that evening's guests, its distance from the action meant the odds were good it would be empty, or at the very least, sparingly used. Matthew figured he could kick out any squatters.

After all, there had to be some advantages to being the guest of honor.

When they got there, they found what Matthew guessed was probably a high-school aged boy dressed as a pirate and a similarly aged girl dressed as a ladybug wrapped around each other on the room's leather sofa. The moment Noel and he entered the room, the couple sprang apart and looked as if they wished the cushions they were sitting on might actually swallow them both whole.

"Do you mind?" Matthew asked, a friendly smile in place. No need to upset the kids any more than was absolutely necessary. "We were kind of hoping to play a game."

"No, no, you go right ahead," the pirate urged, grabbing the now blushing ladybug's hand and hurrying her from the room. Matthew trailed after them, and pulled the door closed once they were gone. Just to be safe, he also flipped the lock.

The room now secure, he turned to look at Noel, who smiled back at him, seemingly amused by the proceedings.

"Should we feel guilty, do you think?" Noel asked. "Thwarting true love?"

"Thwarting underage groping is more like it," Matthew said, pulling a triangle from the wall hook and getting started racking the balls. "Their parents will thank us. Besides, there are plenty of other places to choose from if they want to be alone. Let them find one of those. This is ours."

Noel didn't dispute the claim. Though he did look away, his smile lingering, his cheeks darkening with what Matthew thought might be the beginnings of a blush.

God. Matthew couldn't decide if he wanted to pinch the guy's cheek or his ass. He was really almost too adorable.

"You can get comfortable if you want," Matthew said once the balls were snug in their triangle and in place on the table. As if to show Noel how it was done, he slipped off his biker jacket and laid it over the back of one of the room's chairs. The room was decorated in classic old boys' club style—paneled walls, dark wood, and plenty of tufted leather furniture. Its centerpiece was an intricately carved vintage table his father had picked up at an estate sale years before. "It's just the two of us here. And you might find it's easier to play."

"All right," Noel said after a moment's hesitation, removing his hat and laying it on the end table, before tackling the buttons on his jacket.

Matthew watched the striptease for a moment before suggesting in admittedly far too offhanded a voice. "You know, you could also take off that mask if you feel like it."

Noel looked over, smiled slightly and shook his head. "I don't think that's such a good idea."

Matthew held out his hands, quick to appease. "All right. No pressure. No pressure." Turning away, he got rid of the triangle and put it back on the wall, then removed two cues from their places alongside it. When he turned back, he noticed Noel was now the one watching him, dressed in his uniform pants and a pressed white shirt. He'd loosened the tie around his neck, and was rolling up his sleeves, revealing tan, muscled forearms.

Watching as every inch of golden skin was revealed, Matthew got the sudden urge to take a bite out of one of them.

Instead, he took a deep breath and handed Noel one of the cues. "Ready?"

"Not really," Noel said, chuckling as he took it from him. "What the heck do I do?"

"Let me show you," Matthew said, bending over the table to make the break and get the game underway.

At first, Matthew played the role of the patient instructor, explaining the rules of pool and showing Noel the proper way to hold the cue and line up his shot.

"That's right," Matthew said, standing behind Noel as he prepared to take his first turn. "Straighten your back and kind of push your hips out so you're flat rather than hunched over. Good. Like that."

And if such instruction not only improved Noel's form, but allowed Matthew a singular view, well...

...sometimes things just worked out that way.

At first, the conversation reminded Matthew of a pinball game—one minute they were talking pool; the next, Matthew's experiences at UT, the trip he'd just returned from, or what his plans might be for the future.

But no matter the topic, Noel proved an excellent listener, real when it came to his interest and enthusiasm, and quick to interject with questions or observations of his own.

As a pool player, however, no one would mistake him for anything other than a beginner. Even with a couple of games under his belt, he still didn't really have a feel yet for things like angles, setting up the shot, or even the proper force to be used when making contact, cue to ball. As a result, more often than not, Noel stood on the sidelines watching while Matthew was the one taking his turn. Much as he was enjoying the opportunity to show off a bit, Matthew wanted to make sure his guest wasn't getting bored.

"So tell me about yourself," he urged, glancing up to see Noel's eyes trained on him, one hand on his cue, the other holding a second beer. In addition to everything else, the room had a wet bar. No wonder Matthew's father spent so much time there.

"Not much to tell, really," Noel said, taking a sip of the Corona. "What do you want to know?"

Matthew squatted down to get a closer look at the shot he was getting ready to attempt. "I don't know. Everything. Are you still in school?"

"Ah...no. No. I work."

"Oh, yeah? What do you do?"

"Whatever needs to be done."

That drew Matthew's gaze back to him. "What do you mean?"

Noel shrugged and set aside his beer. "I help out at my family's place. They've got a lot of land and horses, so there's always something that needs doing. I keep busy."

Matthew stood, the game of pool forgotten. "You're from around here?"

"Yeah. Not too far."

"Why don't I know you?"

Noel's attention dipped to the table then back up again. "Actually, we did meet. Years ago. I was just a kid. So I'm sure you don't remember."

Matthew searched his memory. But Noel was right—he couldn't recall any such meeting. "What's your family's name?"

Neal suddenly looked nervous. "I...uh, I don't think you'd know it."

Matthew came around the corner of the table, drawing closer to Noel, his eyes narrowed in speculation. "Yes, you do. But for some reason, you don't want me to know it."

"What—?" Noel began, his posture becoming more alert. "W-why would you say that?"

"Do you deny it?" Matthew asked. "We've done nothing but talk since we came in here. I've told you everything about myself. But you—you haven't said much. I don't know any more about you now than I did when I first saw you."

Noel didn't respond.

"Why all the secrecy?" Matthew asked, trying hard to sound merely curious, rather than accusatory or hurt. "You know you don't have to be mysterious to pique my interest, don't you? I'm already intrigued."

Noel looked at him in disbelief. "Why, though?"

"Why what?"

"Why would you be intrigued by me?"

"Are you kidding me?" Matthew said, leaning his cue against the table so his hands were free. "Have you looked in the mirror recently?"

Noel cocked his head. "What's that supposed to mean?"

"It means you're gorgeous," Matthew said, deciding to go for broke. He was almost certain Noel was as attracted to him as he was to Noel. But even if he were wrong, it was probably better to make his intentions known. "Even with that stupid mask on, I took one look at you and realized I wanted to get to know you better."

Noel laughed, one quick chuff of sound, then pulled back and rested his cue against the wall. "I'm not... You're crazy. I'm not the one who's gorgeous. You...you're the one—" He gestured in Matthew's direction, his hands flailing. Yet Matthew understood his meaning.

Lips quirking with humor, he took a step towards Noel and playfully grabbed hold of his tie. "You think I'm gorgeous, Noel?" he asked, looking into the other man's eyes. He could see color creeping up from under Noel's collar to stain first his neck, then his face. Matthew wanted to press his lips against Noel's blushing skin to see if it felt as warm as it appeared.

Noel avoided his gaze and frowned. "What if I do?"

Matthew pretended to think it over. "Well, let's see—you think I'm gorgeous. I think you are too. We're both consenting adults, alone in a locked room. What to do, what to do, what to do..."

Still smiling, Matthew tugged gently on Noel's tie to pull him nearer. Noel went willingly enough. Yet when Matthew leaned in, he thought perhaps he saw something like worry lurking in Noel's shadowed eyes.

"Don't be afraid," he murmured.

Noel swallowed hard. "I'm not."

"Prove it." With that, Matthew closed the distance and covered Noel's lips with his own, the pressure light, more an invitation than a demand.

Noel allowed the kiss, his mouth warm and slightly chapped beneath Matthew's. Still he didn't reciprocate and his hands remained at his sides.

"It's even better if you kiss me back," Matthew said quietly, reaching up to lay his palm against Noel's cheek, his eyes yet closed.

"Don't laugh," Noel whispered, his breath washing across Matthew's face.

"What?" Matthew said, opening his eyes, certain Noel was joking. Only that wasn't what he saw. Instead, Noel stared back at him, his eyes shining where they peered out at Matthew from behind the mask, his brow drawn with concern.

"What is it?" Matthew asked, his thumb sweeping along Noel's cheekbone, tracing its line, the hand that had been hanging on to Noel's tie, now resting flat against his chest. "What's wrong? Don't you want this?"

"I do," Noel said. And Matthew believed him. "So much."

Matthew took a deep breath, relieved beyond all measure he hadn't misread things. "Then what?"

Noel looked down and wet his lips with his tongue before he spoke. "I just don't want you to be disappointed."

"With you?" Matthew asked, his eyebrows flying towards his hairline as if launched from a springboard.

Noel bobbed his head, his eyes yet averted.

"Not a chance," Matthew promised, his other hand coming up now to capture Noel's face between his palms. "I've wanted you from the first moment I saw you."

Noel looked at him with wonder. "Really?"

"Yeah," Matthew said, nodding once, sharp and sure. "Really."

Noel smiled, the stretch of his lips slight, yet genuine.

Matthew grinned back; his voice was light and teasing. "So do you think you could maybe stop being so neurotic, and just kiss me already?"

Noel's smile widened, his dimples coming out in full force. "Okay."

Hesitating no longer, Noel curled one hand around the back of Matthew's neck and the other around his waist, pulling Matthew against his body and into his embrace. Matthew flowed easily into his arms, his weight driving Noel backwards until he came to rest, leaning against the edge of the pool table. There, he opened his legs and Matthew came to stand between them.

Their mouths met. Noel's lips were parted now and as warm as Matthew remembered. He nudged against them, pressing and releasing, sucking softly on them, above and below, coaxing Noel to respond.

With a gasp, he did, returning the caresses, his kisses sweet, like the kind kids exchange.

Matthew wanted more.

"Let go," he whispered when they parted for the briefest of seconds. He captured Noel's head between his hands, nuzzled at the hollow just in front of Neal's ear, kissed the corner of his mouth, nibbled along his jaw line. "Come on. Don't hold back."

Noel whimpered, then tightened his grip, his arms locked around Matthew's back, his mouth chasing after Matthew's, like the law after a known criminal. Matthew let himself be caught.

This time, when their lips met and clung, Matthew took advantage of Noel's eagerness, and slipped his tongue into his mouth. Noel startled at the contact. But Matthew's hands kept him from pulling away, his fingers clenching in Noel's long hair to hold him steady.

It didn't take Noel long to adjust. Making a sound low in the back of his throat, he relaxed into the new, more intimate kiss, his tongue gliding firmly, his mouth moving over and against Matthew's in a heated, restless rhythm.

God. This was good, Matthew thought, tracing the width of Noel's shoulders, squeezing the dense muscle there and feeling it give against his fingertips. Really good. He didn't know why

Noel had seemed so reluctant at first. He was a natural at this kind of thing, generous and responsive. So much so, his responses were fueling Matthew's own. Noel's hands hadn't even dipped below the waist yet. Still, Matthew could feel himself hardening, his need growing, becoming harder to control.

He would have given anything just then to have Noel spread out beneath him, to have the time to discover what touch was best to make him moan or beg. To experience what Noel's body felt like as it is opened up around him, then closed, tight and hot and clinging. To hear his name whispered by a voice made ragged by need.

But they didn't have that luxury just then. Not with a houseful of guests and his parents only a closed door away. No. Not that night, but another.

Because Matthew planned on seeing Noel again. Every bit of him. He knew that this, this taste, would never be enough. He wanted more. Now all he had to do was get Noel to agree.

Matthew's hands mapped Noel's broad chest, his thumbs finding two peaked nipples and flicking gently there, until Noel twisted from the attention and whined with pleasure. Pulling his mouth away to chuckle before capturing Noel's ear lobe between his teeth, Matthew let his fingers drift down to release Noel's belt from its buckle, to pop free the button at his fly and lower the zipper there.

"How do you like it?" he muttered, pushing inside Noel's clothing to take hold of him. Noel's skin was feverish and silky, its softness a marked contrast to the rigid organ it covered. Matthew stroked the length once to get familiar with it, to feel it pulse and glide against his palm.

"Ah! Anything..." Noel said, his eyes squeezed shut.

Loving the way Noel surrendered to his touch, Matthew played with him some more, keeping his grip light and lazy, enough to keep him interested, but not enough to bring him off.

Noel was trembling now, his face buried against Matthew's neck, his hands roaming as if desperate for the contact, touching every bit of Matthew he could reach.

"Matthew," he whispered, his voice sounding so lost that

Matthew wondered if he even realized he was speaking at all. "Please...oh, please..."

Christ. Matthew honestly couldn't remember the last time someone had wanted him this badly. Especially not when their reaction was being fueled by something as simple as a handjob. It was heady stuff. And a little scary, to have that much power over someone so willingly vulnerable.

And suddenly, Matthew didn't want to draw it out any longer, didn't want to tease, not when Noel was being so open, and so obviously trusting.

He took his free hand and worked open the fly on his jeans. Reaching under his clothing, he pulled out his swollen cock and, switching his grip, gathered it up alongside Noel's, closing his fingers around them both.

"Yeah," he groaned, teeth gritted, closing his eyes and pressing his forehead against Noel's cheek. Noel's arms circled around him, holding him close.

Matthew used the moisture their bodies were secreting to ease his way, allowing him to slide down smoothly, his knuckles skating against Noel's firm belly, then back up again, his grip tight, the pace steady.

Together, Noel and he bucked and panted and clung to one another as if to do otherwise would end in world-destroying disaster until finally Noel's hips snapped forward and his head tilted back.

"Fuck," Noel said brokenly, shuddering as he spilled all over Matthew's hand.

The warmth and wetness flowing over Matthew's skin was enough to finish him off as well, and with another couple of thrusts, he let go, muffling his cry against the base of Noel's throat.

They stood there together in the aftermath, just holding each other, each a little unsteady on their feet. Noel's hands were drawing random patterns across Matthew's back, his cheek rested heavy and hot against the side of Matthew's head.

"Thank you," Noel said softly after a time, pressing a kiss to Matthew's temple, his hand coming up to scratch lightly through Matthew's hair. "That was..." He shook his head before kissing Matthew again, this time on the forehead. "Thanks. I'll never forget it."

Matthew looked up at him, wondering at his mood. Noel's skin was flushed and glowing; sweat beaded at his hairline. Gazing out from behind the mask he still wore, his eyes were more pupil than anything, but Matthew thought the color edging all that black might be brown or hazel. After what they'd just shared, he was surprised to see a kind of sadness shining there.

"You okay?" Matthew asked, worried.

Noel chuckled, but any actual humor seemed to be missing. "Oh yeah. A little messy," he said, looking down at where his pants were rucked and spread open. "But I'm okay."

Matthew eased himself from Noel's arms and hitched up his jeans. "I think I can help with that." Crossing to the wet bar, he grabbed a rag lying crumpled on the counter there. After doing a cursory clean-up job of his own, he tossed the frayed bit of toweling to Noel. "Here you go."

Noel caught it and got started putting his own appearance to rights. "Thanks."

As he got himself together, Matthew watched Noel clean himself off and zip up his pants. He had just begun to roll down his sleeves, when Matthew asked, "So when can I see you again?"

Noel stopped what he was doing and looked up at Matthew through his bangs. "What?"

"I want to see you again," Matthew said, coming over to him. "We could make an evening out of it. You know...dinner, go to a movie or whatever. We could even drive down to Dallas if you want, spend the night."

Noel frowned and began working a little faster at putting his costume back together. "I...um...I don't think that's such a good idea."

"Why not?" Matthew asked, unexpectedly hurt by Noel's response. He didn't understand it. He knew Noel liked him, had liked what they'd just done together. So why was he suddenly playing coy?

"It's just—" Noel avoided Matthew's eyes as he buttoned the

cuff on his shirt. "There are some things about me you don't know."

"Yeah," Matthew said, stopping just short of rolling his eyes. "Lots of things. Because you won't talk to me."

That made Noel look at him. "I'm trying to protect you."

"From what?" Matthew said, spreading his arms wide as if to urge this unknown enemy to take his best shot. "In case you haven't noticed, I'm big boy, and not without my resources. I can take care of myself."

Noel was all but strangling himself as he tried to straighten his tie. "Yeah...well, maybe you're right, and you can take care of yourself. Maybe I'm just protecting me."

Matthew took a step towards him. "What are you talking about?"

"Matthew, look at us," Noel urged. "You have everything going for you. You're a college graduate. You've got money, looks—"

"Yeah," Matthew said dryly, unused to having to work this hard to get someone to go out with him. "Most people would consider me an excellent catch."

"You are," Noel agreed, nodding. "I know that. You could have anyone."

"I want you," Matthew said, curling his fingers in the belt loops of Noel's pants and pulling him close. "That's what I'm trying to tell you."

Noel sighed and bowed his head. Reaching down, he gently took Matthew's hands in his own. "Maybe tonight. Maybe even for a while." He raised his chin and looked Matthew in the eye. "But not once you knew what you were getting yourself into." He squeezed Matthew's fingers in his grasp. "I'm nobody. And you deserve so much more."

Matthew felt as if his brain were short-circuiting. He didn't know if he'd ever been told by someone he was pursuing that they weren't good enough for him. Most of his prospective dates took great pains to convince him of exactly the opposite. "I don't—"

Noel stopped him with a kiss, one that was tender and lasting, and made Matthew want to grab hold of him and never let go.

"This has been the best night of my life," Noel said softly when their lips had parted, and Matthew's face was cradled between his palms. "I want you to know that."

"Then stay," Matthew urged, his hands covering Noel's. He knew all kinds of important things were going unsaid between them, but for the life of him he could begin to figure out how to begin such a conversation. "I want you to stay."

"I can't," Noel said, easing free of Matthew's hold. "In fact... What time is it?"

Matthew glanced at the wall clock behind the bar. "Five till twelve."

Noel paled. "Oh, my God. I've got to get out of here."

Matthew grabbed hold of his arm when Noel reached past to retrieve his jacket. "What's your hurry? Your coach going to turn into a pumpkin or something?"

"No," Noel said, shrugging into his uniform coat. "It's just...it's later than I'd thought."

"Late?" Matthew said. "My mom paid the deejay to play until two. There's plenty of party left."

"Not for me," Noel said, nearly running for the door.

Matthew was right on his heels. "Hold on a second! At least let me walk you out—"

Together, they burst from the billiards room into the hallway, startling the handful of people gathered there, chatting. Dillon was among them.

Noel took one look at the tall, dark vampire and stumbled, putting his hand against the wall to catch himself. "Shit," he breathed with the kind of horror Dillon's costume really didn't deserve, and bolted past the group towards the kitchen.

Trapped in the tangle of guests, Matthew called after him, "Wait!"

Only Noel didn't listen. He yanked open one of the patio doors and nearly threw himself through it, escaping into the night.

Not ready to give up just yet, Matthew tried to shoulder past, only to feel a hand close over his wrist, holding him back.

"Matthew, who was that?"

Matthew turned around to see Dillon looking at him with concern.

"His name is Noel," Matthew said, cursing himself, Noel, and most especially Dillon, for keeping them apart.

"What did he say to you?" Dillon asked, releasing Matthew now that he had his attention.

"Not much," Matthew said, frowning. "Why? Do you know him?"

Matthew had never thought of Dillon as the sort who got rattled easily, but he sure as hell looked unnerved by something just then. "I...I thought I did. Only now I'm not so sure."

"Who is he?" Matthew asked, grabbing hold of Dillon by the arms and leaning in close. Those who had been standing nearby, visiting with Dillon, melted away, giving the two men their privacy. "He wouldn't tell me his last name or how to reach him."

For some reason, that seemed to make Dillon breathe easier. Sighing, he shook his head. "I don't know that I could help you with that either. I think he's a guy I might have run into at a party in Dallas over the summer. But it's hard to tell. I didn't really get a good look at him just now."

Bitterly disappointed, Matthew nodded and let go of the other man. "Yeah. I can see how it might be tough. You only caught a glimpse of him, and he was wearing that ridiculous mask."

"Yeah," Dillon agreed, although it seemed as if he weren't really paying attention to Matthew anymore. He was looking instead in the direction Noel had run. "Sorry. Matthew, would you excuse me? I need to go check and see how my mom and sister are faring."

Oh, that's right. The whole family would be there. Matthew could recall earlier in the evening catching sight of Elaine dressed as some kind of Greek goddess and Lucy wearing a genie costume. "Sure. Thanks, man," he said, watching as, with a wave, Dillon walked away.

Not really wanting to return to the party, yet not knowing what else to do with himself, Matthew went back inside the billiards room.

The first thing he saw was Noel's hat, lying forgotten on the end table.

"Oh, Christ," Matthew mumbled to himself as he walked over and picked up the cap. "You really are Cinderella." For a moment, he let his fingers trace the hat's black brim, its bright gold insignia and braid, before tossing the headwear onto the couch and plopping himself down beside it. With a sigh, he buried his head in his hands.

"Well, aren't you just the life of the party."

Matthew looked up and saw Cal standing in the doorway. "Where's your harem?"

Cal strolled into the room, looking around as if trying to guess what might have prompted Matthew's black mood. "Mia left me for another man and Abby decided to be a good daughter and make an early night of it. Apparently her father, the reverend, expects her to be at sunrise service tomorrow morning. Got her phone number though for when we're up in New York playing at Banjo Jim's. So all is not lost."

Matthew nodded, still unsmiling. "I hope she didn't tell her father about her gig as a dancing ho. It'd break the man's heart."

"Funny you should mention that," Cal said, throwing himself into the club chair opposite and crossing his booted feet on the coffee table almost directly in front of Matthew. "Your long face has heartbreak written all over it. What the hell is going on?"

"I met someone," Matthew said.

"Which is usually a good thing," Cal replied. When Matthew said nothing further, he continued, "Do I need to lay down some hurt?"

Matthew arched his brow. "Are you offering to defend my virtue?"

Cal shrugged. "Such as it is."

"Well, don't worry," Matthew said, falling back against the couch cushions and tilting his chin towards the ceiling. "My virtue is intact. Mostly. It's my ego that's taken a hit."

"Don't tell me you got turned down?"

"Abandoned is more like it," Matthew said, looking at him. "I don't know what I said or what I did. But he ran out of here like he had rockets on his heels."

"Who's 'he'?" Cal asked.

"That's just it," Matthew said, pressing to his feet and heading in the direction of the bar. Maybe it was time for him to move on from beer to something stronger. "I don't know who he is!"

"What?" Cal asked. "You messed around with some guy wearing a mask?"

Matthew stopped and looked over his shoulder at him.

"Aw, hell," Cal said and started laughing.

"Fuck you, I'm heartbroken," Matthew growled, turning to face his friend. He'd said the words to try and be amusing. Only he'd be the first to admit—they hadn't come out sounding all that funny.

Apparently recognizing there must be more truth to his statement than Matthew had wanted to let on, Cal sobered quickly and said, "Tell me what happened."

Sparing Cal any intimate details, Matthew took a seat on the coffee table and recounted how he'd spent the last few hours with Noel, what had been said, and how strangely things had ended.

When he had finished, Cal swung his legs off the table and put his feet flat on the floor. Leaning forward in his chair, his fingers laced, he looked at Matthew. "Son, sounds to me like you need to go after that boy."

Matthew frowned, not sure if he should be amazed or annoyed by Cal's advice. "What—now?"

"No, not now," Cal said, standing. "Don't be stupid."

"Oh, and chasing after a guy I practically begged to go out with me would be the height of intelligence," Matthew said, standing again himself, "especially when I don't even know where to find him."

"You afraid of a little detective work?" Cal asked. "You know the guy's first name. You know pretty much what he looks like, and you know he lives around here. How hard can it be to track him down? You could get started first thing in the morning."

Matthew sighed. "Cal, look—I really don't feel like putting on my official Hardy Boys secret decoder ring. Okay? And I sure as hell am not ready to appear that desperate."

"You know," Cal said, folding his arms, "as good-looking as you are, I never would have believed you put much stock in appearances."

Glaring at his friend, Matthew turned and started towards the bar again. If any conversation merited a shot or two of his father's favorite Añejo tequila, it appeared this one would.

"I know I'm going to regret asking this," Matthew said, pulling the bottle and two shot glasses out from under the bar. "But what the hell are you talking about?"

"I'm talking about you being unwilling to go the extra mile for someone I can tell you care about," Cal said, coming to stand opposite him.

"Oh yeah," Matthew said, pouring them each a shot. "Because being repeatedly rejected is way more fun than most people realize."

"Don't be such a baby," Cal said, leaning in on his elbow. "And think for a second beyond your hurt feelings."

Matthew slammed his shot, wishing he had a lime to chase it with, and wiped the back of his hand over his mouth. "A few more of those, and I won't be thinking anything at all."

"Cut it out," Cal said, whacking him none too gently on the shoulder. "You'll need your head in the game tomorrow morning if you're gonna find your Prince Charming."

"Cinderella," Matthew said, pouring himself another shot.

"Whatever," Cal said, sipping at his. "You know I've never understood how this whole gay thing works."

"Yeah?" Matthew said. "Well I don't understand why you're so damned fixated on me going after Noel. I thought you were my friend. Aren't you supposed to take my side?"

"I am taking your side, you idiot," Cal said. "I'm telling you to go after him because you want to. You want him." Looking down at his tequila, Cal shrugged. "And call me a sentimental fool, but I like my friends to get what they want."

Matthew had to smile at that. Because while Cal was no one's fool, he was a big ol' softie when it came to the people he loved.

"But also...because something don't feel right about this."

"What do you mean?" Matthew asked.

"The guy tells you it's the best night of his life, that he'll always remember it, he thanks you for it, and then he leaves you?" Cal said. "What kind of crap is that?"

"Don't forget the part about him wanting to protect me," Matthew murmured, taking a drink of his tequila.

Cal nodded. "Yeah, exactly. The whole thing is weird. So the way I figure it, one of two things is going on here. One, he's married or in a relationship or something, and you were his Halloween fling."

"He wasn't wearing a ring," Matthew said.

"Which only proves he planned ahead," Cal replied.

Matthew inclined his head, conceding that point

"Or he's in some kind of trouble," Cal said, "and is trying to keep you out of it."

Matthew considered that hypothesis. "That seems more likely to me. I just didn't get a cheating vibe off of him. He didn't seem like a player. You know? He was more innocent than that, more naïve."

"So what—you're saying he's no criminal mastermind either?"

"I wouldn't have thought so," Matthew said, shaking his head. "But hell, who knows?"

"You won't," Cal said, "unless you go after him and find out the truth. You know I'm right."

Matthew didn't say anything.

"And you know you want to."

Matthew reached up and scrubbed his face with his palm. "God," he groaned before dropping his hand, and giving Cal a faint smile. "Okay. You know what? You've convinced me. Let's do it."

"Whoa," Cal said, hands held out in front of him. "Who said anything about me being involved in all this?"

"Oh, no," Matthew said, chuckling. "Don't you try and weasel out of it now, not after you were the one who talked me into it in the first place. If I really am going to try and track down Noel, you're going to help me do it."

Laughing now as well, Cal shrugged and toasted Matthew with what was left of his tequila. "All right, all right. I guess that's fair."

"Glad that's settled," Matthew said, finishing off his second shot. "Now which Hardy do you want to be—Frank or Joe?"

~*~*~*~

Bending low over Midnight's neck, Noah gave the stallion his head and simply tried to hang on as they raced for home.

Of course, with the way Noah's heart was pounding, it was a wonder he hadn't already spooked his horse.

God.

First, to have suddenly realized he'd lost all track of time.

Then to have literally run into Dillon when he'd tried to leave.

Talk about screwing things up.

Still, he had to keep reminding himself—it had been dark in that hallway and crowded. Chances were good Dillon hadn't even realized it was him. After all, it wasn't like Noah made a habit of showing up at the same parties his stepbrother frequented. The element of surprise alone should be enough to throw Dillon off the scent.

Better still, even if Dillon had, for some reason, wondered at his identity, Matthew wouldn't have been able to tell him anything. Not anything useful, anyway. Noah didn't think Dillon would automatically put two and two together and come up with him.

At least he hoped Dillon wouldn't.

But even if he did, Noah would never regret the decision he'd made or the night he'd just enjoyed. He'd gone to his first party, drunk his first beer, played his first game of pool...

...and had sex with the man he loved.

Noah wasn't stupid. He knew what Matthew and he had done together was considered pretty tame by most people's standards, only the first step towards something far more intimate. But for him, in that moment, it had been as if the cosmos had been rearranged to spell his name, miles high and galaxies bright, all shimmering and eternal.

To hold and kiss someone he had pined after for years and to be brought by that person to a shattering climax in his arms...

...well, as far as Noah was considered, it didn't get much better than that.

Which was why, terrified as he was, ears, nose and hands all but numb from cold, Noah couldn't stop smiling as Midnight and he hurried home.

As he had done on his way to the party, Noah pulled his horse to a stop before he reached the stable and dismounted.

"Come on, boy," he said, taking the reins and leading Midnight along the narrow dirt path. "We're almost there. We're just going to walk the rest of the way. Quiet now."

It had turned into a cold night for North Texas in autumn. Noah could see steam rising from Midnight's hide and his own breath escaping in misty clouds every time he exhaled.

And to think, he could still have been inside, secreted away with Matthew until dawn, drinking beer and getting to know each other better and better.

But, oh no, Noah thought to himself, eyes on the uneven ground. I had to hurry home.

And to what? A lonely existence on the third floor and a life of drudgery. It had been so tempting to confide in Matthew, to tell him about what his life had been like since coming to Texas and to beg for his help.

But Noah couldn't do it.

I'm already pathetic enough, Noah thought as he hiked along the trail. The last thing I want to do is to make Matthew feel like he needs to rescue me.

After all, Noah loved the guy. You didn't ask something like that from someone you loved.

Knowing the kind of man he was, Noah was pretty sure if Matthew found out about his circumstances, he'd feel honor-bound to help. And if that were to happen, Noah would almost instantly go from someone Matthew was intrigued by to a burden, a thing no sane individual would want anything to do with.

Noah didn't think he could take that, to witness how Matthew's feelings for him would change over time.

Better to have this one precious night, when he'd allowed himself to believe—even if only for a little while—that he was someone Matthew might have a future with.

I'll always have this, Noah thought. No matter what Elaine says or does, she can't take tonight away.

Treading carefully, Noah guided Midnight into the stable

yard. The sliding door was closed and he didn't see any lights beyond those that had been on when he'd left. It appeared he may have escaped detection.

Pushing the barn door on the far side of the stable open just wide enough for both Midnight and him to pass through, Noah brought the horse inside, closing the door after them. "Here we go. Let's get you taken care of."

Noah returned Midnight to his stall, then quickly stripped off his tack and rubbed him down.

"That'll have to do for tonight, buddy. Okay?" he said, gathering everything up so he could put it back in the tack room, where it belonged. "Tomorrow I'll do better by you. I promise. After all, I owe you big-time for not dropping me on my behind." Midnight watched him work and didn't seem to mind.

After putting away the gear, Noah rushed to get himself changed. He didn't want to be seen entering the house in his costume. He'd have a hard enough time explaining why he was up and out if he was caught in his usual clothing.

Once he was dressed again in his typical jeans, long-sleeved checked shirt, and tennis shoes, he folded the uniform and tucked it behind a stack of old crates. It wasn't the cleanest place to hide it. But Noah thought it should escape Willis' attention there.

"I'll be back for you later," Noah murmured, standing and brushing off his hands on his pants' legs.

"Good night, Midnight," he said softly as he walked past the horse's stall on his way out of the stable. "Thanks again for taking care of me."

When he got to the barn door that faced the house, Noah slid it open just a crack to see if he could detect any movement in the yard. He stared hard into the darkness, listened for footsteps or any stirring in the brush. Nothing seemed out of place.

He took a deep breath.

Here goes nothing.

Noah pushed open the door far enough to let him slip through. However, he didn't even clear the doorway before a pair of hands grabbed him and pushed him back inside.

Willis.

He must have been waiting for him outside.

The stable hand closed the door after them both and stood in front of it, his arms folded. When Noah's eyes flicked in the direction of the door opposite, Willis took a couple of steps forward and to the side, effectively blocking access to both exits. "You know what they did to horse thieves in the Old West, boy? They strung 'em up, hung 'em by the neck until dead."

"I didn't steal any horses," Noah said, mind racing as he tried to figure out what to do next. While he was older than the last time he'd faced off against this man, heavier and stronger, he still didn't have much in the way of fighting experience. He feared Willis' knowledge in that area balanced out any physical edge he might have gained.

"No?" Willis said, arching a brow. "That's not what I saw. I saw you walking back, leading that big black stallion you're so fond of. The one I'm pretty damned sure your momma told you to stay away from."

Spotlighted by the bulb overhead, Noah edged his way to the right, trying to get a better angle for escape. "You just said it yourself. I was leading him back. He's in his stall right now. Nobody stole him."

Willis lowered his arms and took a step towards him, forcing Noah to retreat. "If you brought him back, chances are you were the one who took him to begin with. Don't play word games with me—borrow or steal, you rode that horse without permission."

"So what if I did," Noah said. "I didn't hurt anybody. What difference does it make?"

"The difference is you still haven't learned," Willis said, coming closer, his gait beginning to subtly change. He moved easier all of a sudden, more loosely. His knees were bent, his stance was wide.

Noah might not know much about fighting, but he could tell Willis was preparing to strike.

Noah brought his hands up in front of him. He wanted to be

ready.

"I told you years ago," Willis said. "I warned you to keep your nose clean. But you didn't listen. I guess you really are as stupid as I always thought you were."

With no more warning than that, Willis lowered his head and charged, his shoulder hitting Noah at waist level, and driving him back against one of the stable's support posts.

Noah grunted at the impact, knowing his back would be black and blue by morning. But he was able to push Willis off of him before the other man could do any real damage. Willis fell away a few strides and grinned.

"Well, look at the tough guy," he said, fists before him, swaying like he was in the ring. "You may be able to wrestle some. But have you learned to box?"

Willis led with his right. Bracing himself, Noah was able to block the blow with his forearm. But when Willis followed up with his left, he caught Noah on his side, just below the ribs. Gasping, Noah staggered away, breathing hard, but still on his feet.

Willis came at him again, aiming for Noah's middle. Noah curled over and to the side to protect himself, his shoulder taking most of the impact. It hurt, but not enough to incapacitate him.

Still in defensive mode, he swung with his right arm, thinking more about driving Willis back than actually hitting him. Somehow, he got lucky. Noah's fist connected with Willis' cheek, snapping his head to the side and making him stumble away, leaving the path to the door open.

Seeing his opportunity, Noah scrambled for it. But before he could get past him, Willis threw himself after Noah, tackling him around the legs.

"Oh no, you don't."

Noah kicked at him, trying to throw the other man off. But Willis had Noah's legs all but pinned as he crawled up his body.

They spun and clawed on the floor of the stable, throwing punches with more energy than accuracy. The horses began to murmur and stir, frightened by their grappling.

Finally, after another successful blow to his opponent's face,

Noah rolled swiftly to his knees and found himself on top of Willis, straddling him. He pinned Willis' right hand to the ground with his left and pressed his right arm against Willis' throat, tipping back Willis' chin. Willis had the fingers of his left hand wrapped tightly around Noah's arm, doing all he could to pry it off, but Noah had leverage and wouldn't be moved.

If he could just keep up the pressure, Willis should eventually faint, Noah thought, straining to hold the other man immobile. He remembered how quickly he'd gotten lightheaded when Willis had tried a similar move on him the night of the fireworks.

Only Willis wasn't giving up without a fight; Noah had to struggle to hold his position. Sweat dripped from his hairline and down his cheeks, his breath burst from his mouth in harsh, hurried little puffs.

So focused was he on the task at hand, Noah didn't sense the movement behind him until it was too late. Just when he thought he might have spied something, and was turning his head to see what was in back of him, something heavy and hard came down right above his ear. Rocked by the blow, Noah cried out and buckled, falling over onto his side.

Moaning, he lay there dazed, the pain in his head enough to make his stomach roil. He couldn't get his eyes to focus. Everything was blurry and seemed to have a twin. The side of his head was wet and felt as if it had to be twice the size it should be. Noah couldn't remember how he came to be there, lying in a heap on the floor. But he knew it wasn't safe, that he should try and get away.

If only he could recall how to move.

"Son of a bitch! Son of a bitch," someone said from very close by. The person sounded as if they had a cold, their voice hoarse and low. Noah thought the one speaking might be Willis, but he couldn't be sure. "Where the fuck have you been? You called nearly an hour ago."

"I got here as soon as I could. It took us forever to get our car." The second voice sounded to Noah like Dylan. But that couldn't be right. He was still at the party.

Wasn't he?

"Your stepbrother here almost murdered me."

"Guess you're not as tough as you used to be, old man."

"Fuck you. Not everyone has a shovel handy. Give me a hand up."

Noah heard rustling not far from where he lay, then an awful sounding groan. He wondered for a moment if he might have been the one responsible for making it. A shadow fell over him.

"You're gonna wish you had killed me, kid."

All at once, agony exploded low in Noah's belly, something dull and heavy walloping him there. He writhed and rolled, desperate to avoid it, his mobility all at once restored. Another wicked blow hit him almost on top of the first, making him curl in a ball to protect the tender spot. Then a third struck him in the back, forcing his spine to arch and a scream to tear from his throat.

"Enough. Stop kicking him! If you're not careful, you'll be the one killing somebody."

"I don't care."

"You may not. But my mother does."

"Your mother is crazy. I told her this was a bad idea. She's let it go on way too long."

"That's not your call. Come on. We need to get him out of sight until we figure out what to do."

Noah wasn't aware of much, but he felt two sets of hands grab hold of his arms and drag him across the floor. The movement jarred his injuries. He gasped as the pain flared like bonfires beneath his skin, and tried to lift his head. Only it was too heavy for him to hoist, so he had to let it hang, his chin tapping out code against his chest.

"In here. This ought to do for now," said the gruffer voice.

Noah heard a door open. Then he was dropped and pushed none too gently against a hard wooden wall.

"Tie his wrists. Better get his feet too," said the other.

Rough hands pulled Noah's arms behind him and bound them with rope. His ankles were similarly secured.

"One more thing," the first voice said.

Someone's fingers clenched near his scalp, and pulled Noah

upright by his hair. Eyes watering, he opened his mouth to protest, only to have a crumpled piece of cloth shoved between his lips, and another tied over the wad to hold it in place.

"I'd try not to be sick if I were you," that same voice said. "I'd hate for you to choke to death on your own vomit."

The thought of that end was enough to do what all the previous damage hadn't. With a muffled sob, Noah closed his eyes and succumbed to the darkness, content that at least in some small way he would finally be able to escape.

"Of all the asinine ideas you've come up with over the years—I can't believe I let you talk me into this one."

"What are you complaining about? At least if this works, you're going to get a boyfriend out of it. The best I can hope for is the satisfaction that comes from a job well done."

Chuckling, Matthew shook his head, looked over at Cal, and sighed. "Not exactly the best way to spend a Sunday, is it?"

Dressed in jeans and a red flannel shirt, Cal drove, his hand steady on the wheel of his truck. He shrugged. "Could be worse. At least the Cowboys aren't playing."

They'd set off just after breakfast, taking with them a map of the surrounding area, and Noel's forgotten hat. The plan had been to knock on doors, starting with those closest to Valley View, gradually widening their search until they found their man.

Right off the bat, they'd hit a few snags. First of all, while neither Cal nor Matthew were churchgoers, most of Matthew's neighbors were. They'd discovered few people home before noon.

Secondly, while they wanted to keep their search pattern as controlled as possible, they weren't able to pursue it in as systematic a manner as Matthew would have liked. They didn't live in Manhattan, after all, and the roads in this part of Texas weren't exactly laid out in a grid. They'd begun by heading west. But after driving nearly twenty miles along the main county road and having nothing to show for it, they'd doubled back east, thinking they'd try the other direction, hitting houses they'd missed along the way.

No one they'd talked to so far had ever heard of a man named Noel, nor had anyone who had attended the party recalled seeing him there.

"What time is it?" Cal asked.

Matthew checked his watch. "Three o'clock."

"What do you say we give it until five," Cal said. "Then you and me knock off, go get a couple of steaks and a pitcher of beer, kick back, and start fresh again tomorrow morning."

"Tomorrow is Monday," Matthew said, rubbing his hand over his face.

"Yes, and the day after will be Tuesday. Your point?"

"My point is not everyone has the same luxury as you and me. Some people actually work for a living."

"I work."

"In theory."

"Fuck you."

"All I'm saying is we might be wasting our time during the workweek. More than we already have, I mean."

Cal glanced his way. "Do you really believe that, that this is an exercise in futility?"

Matthew looked out the window on his side, his eyes narrowed against the late afternoon sun. "I don't know. It just feels so...pointless. You know? Like we're searching for a needle in a haystack." He looked over at Cal.

"We kinda are," Cal said, the corner of his mouth turning up. "But it's only been a few hours, Matt. Try and have a little faith."

Taking a deep breath, Matthew shoved aside his pessimism and smiled. "All right. I'll try. But I'm not making any promises."

Cal nodded his understanding as they zipped past the entrance to Valley View. "Where to next?" he asked.

Matthew didn't even need to consult their map. "The folks next door are on vacation. I know because we're babysitting their plants. So that means Dillon and his family are next."

Cal grinned. "You showing up on his doorstep unannounced ought to give him quite a thrill."

"Maybe he'll be back at school already."

"Not with the luck you've been having."

"At least you're here to protect me," Matthew said, only partially joking. "You should have seen him last night. At one point, he cornered me in the library and started talking about vampire erotica. I know he was going for titillating, but it was all I could do not to laugh in his face."

"Seems to me that boy's face could stand to be laughed in more often."

Matthew chuckled. "I don't know. He's handsome enough."

"Agreed," Cal said easily enough. "What he lacks in personality, he more than makes up for in looks. Good thing you're not shallow."

"Oh, don't worry. I'd have to be puddle deep to show any interest in Dillon."

"Well, with any luck, we can be in and out of there quick."

"Maybe not so quick," Matthew said. "Last night, Dillon seemed to think he might have seen Noah before. Maybe he's remembered where."

They turned into the property's entrance, and drove until they came to the cheery yellow and white home. Just as Cal was turning off the engine, Elaine appeared on the porch to greet them.

"Good afternoon, boys," she said, looking elegant and stylish in dove gray slacks, a white twin set and pearls. "What can I do for you?"

"Hi," Matthew said as he got out of the truck. Cal grabbed the bag holding Noel's hat, before exiting as well, and came to stand beside him, a solid, reassuring presence. He said nothing, allowing Matthew take the lead. "We were wondering—are Dillon and Lucy home? I need to ask y'all something about last night."

Elaine's eyebrows rose in surprise; yet that was the only emotion she betrayed. "Yes, they are. Come on inside. I'll fix you both some coffee."

Climbing the front steps, the two men followed her into the

house.

"Dillon? Lucy! Come in to the living room," Elaine called from the foyer. "Matthew and a friend are here. They want to talk to you about last night!"

Smiling a polite, if not particularly warm smile, she led her guests into a lavishly appointed room. Matthew had been to the house before, of course. But the last time he'd visited, all he'd done was trail after Dillon into the kitchen. He hadn't really looked around, or paid much attention to his surroundings. Now that he did, he saw expensive, almost feminine furnishings that appeared as if they'd never been sat on or touched. Matthew felt underdressed in his jeans, henley, and leather jacket, like he should be wearing a suit before being allowed to set foot in the place.

"Hey, Matthew," Dillon said, all but beaming as he entered from the direction of the kitchen. He offered Matthew his hand, which Matthew took. "What's going on?"

Matthew was about to answer when he saw Lucy coming down the stairs.

"Hi, Matthew." The teenager smiled shyly at him when she reached the foyer, giving a little wave before walking past him into the living room. Both siblings were dressed in jeans and sweaters.

"Why don't you all have a seat?" Elaine suggested. "I'll go get a pot of coffee started."

"Actually, I don't know that we need coffee," Matthew said, looking over at Cal, who shook his head. "And I'd really like you to be here for this too, if you don't mind."

"Of course." Elaine sat down on one of the room's chintz slipper chairs. Her children followed suit by sitting across from her on the matching sofa. Matthew and Cal remained standing. "Whatever you need," she said. "We're happy to help."

"I appreciate that." Matthew ran his hand over his head before he spoke. "Last night, there was a guy at our party. Someone I'd never met before. He's not in trouble or anything. But I'm trying to find him, and he didn't give me his last name or his number. All I know is he supposedly lives near here."

"Why do you think we might know him?" Elaine asked, her

hands folded neatly on her lap.

"I don't know that you specifically know him," Matthew said. "We're asking everyone who was at the party and lives in the vicinity. I figure someone has to know who this guy is."

"What does he look like?" Lucy asked.

"He was dressed as a military officer and wearing this." Matthew looked over to Cal who pulled Noel's hat from the bag and showed it around. Matthew watched the reactions of the three people he was questioning. The hat seemed to have no impact on Lucy. However, he noticed Dillon shared a quick glance with his mother before once again focusing on Matthew and what he was saying.

"He told me his first name was Noel," Matthew continued. "He was really tall, maybe six-two or three, young—I'm guessing college-aged. He had long dark brown hair. I didn't get a good look at them, but his eyes may have been brown or hazel. He was wearing a mask. Does that ring any bells?"

Lucy shook her head. "I don't think so, but I kind of hung out by the deejay all night. Was this guy dancing?"

"No," Matthew said. "He spent most of the evening playing pool with me."

"Then no," Lucy said. "I'm pretty sure I wouldn't have seen him. Sorry."

"What about you, Dillon?" Matthew said, coming to stand in front of the other man. "I know you saw him. In fact, at the time, you seemed to think you recognized him. Were you able to figure out where you knew him from?"

Dillon looked up at him, his eyes shining with what looked like regret, and shrugged. "No. I'm sorry, man. It's like I said last night—I'd thought the guy looked familiar. But I couldn't tell you why. Maybe he's someone I know from school."

"No, I don't think so," Matthew said. "He said he wasn't in school. That he was working at his family's place. He mentioned something about horses and made it sound like wherever it was, it had to be around here."

"That's not much to go on, hon," Elaine said, her expression sympathetic. "Nearly everyone around here keeps horses."

"Yeah," Matthew said, nodding and looking down at the floor.

"I know." God. He'd really hoped Dillon would be the one to solve the mystery. He'd seemed so certain last night that he'd seen Noel before. Now, if only he could remember where...

"How 'bout you, Ma'am?" Cal asked, speaking for the first time. "I saw you at the party last night, looking lovely, may I add. Do you recall seeing this boy?"

"No, I don't think so," Elaine said, shaking her head. "But there were so many people there. I'm sure he could have come and gone without my catching sight of him."

Matthew sighed. Another dead end. "All right. Well...thanks for your time." He reached down to take Elaine's slim, cool hand in both of his. "And if you remember anything or talk to anyone who does, please give me a call. You've got my mom's number."

"You've got it," Dillon said, standing. "Let me walk you out."

Lucy and Elaine stayed behind in the living room as the three men headed for the door.

"Hey," Dillon said when they reached the foyer. "I was gonna head back to school today. But after getting in so late last night, I decided to stay an extra day or two. I'm free tonight if you want to do something."

Matthew glanced at Cal. Cal looked back at him, lips twitching as he tried not to smile. "Thanks, but, ah...sorry. I've already got plans."

"Oh," Dillon said, his brows drawing together. "Okay. Well, maybe next time I'm in town. Why don't you give me your cell number? That way, if—"

Before Dillon could finish his thought, he was interrupted by a booming crash from overhead.

"What the hell?" Cal murmured, peering up at the ceiling above as if he thought it might come crumbling down on top of him.

"That sounded like someone fell down the stairs," Matthew said, looking over at Dillon, expecting he would know the cause. The other man looked back, his eyes wide, saying nothing. All color had been leeched from his face; his cheeks were paler than they'd been the night before when he'd been made up as a vampire.

"I'm sure something just fell over up there," Elaine said, standing in the living room doorway. She too appeared agitated, her hand coming up to pluck restlessly at the buttons on her cardigan, her lips pressed thin. Behind her, Lucy watched everyone with wide eyes.

The family's odd reaction was enough to make Matthew curious. "Better check it out," he said, starting up the stairs.

"No!" Dillon cried, grabbing on to Matthew's arm to try and hold him back.

"Don't you want to see what that was?" Matthew asked, having no intention of backing down regardless of Dillon's answer.

"We'll take care of it," Elaine said, coming to stand beside her son.

"Don't worry, Ma'am," Cal said, his foot on the bottom step, mischief in his eyes. "We're happy to check it out for you. Come on, Matt." Grinning, he started up the stairs.

Pulling free of Dillon's grip, Matthew followed.

"Wait!" Dillon called before charging up the staircase after them.

When they reached the second floor, Matthew didn't immediately see what could have caused the noise. Then he heard something filtering through a closed door at the end of the hall.

"Help!"

Sharing a look, Matthew and Cal ran towards the sound. Dillon was right behind them at the top of the stairs.

When he got to the door, Matthew pulled it open. Before he could investigate what was hidden behind it, something heavy and metal tumbled free at his feet, making him dance out of the way. He glanced down.

A walker, like senior citizens or invalids used.

"Help me, please."

Looking up, Matthew saw the door led to an additional flight of stairs. There, at the top of them, was a woman. She was frail and old, clothed in a dressing gown and slippers. She sat, her weight resting on her hip, her hand stretched out towards him. Even with the distance separating them, Matthew could see it trembling.

"No, you can't go up there!" Dillon was right behind him.

"Oh, why don't you shut up?" Cal said.

Already on his way up the stairs, Matthew heard the thump of fist hitting face, then a thud. It sounded like Cal had the situation under control.

"Ma'am, are you all right?" Matthew asked as he neared the top.

"Yes," she said, nodding. "Y-yes. But you must help my grandson."

"Is he up here with you?" Matthew asked, reaching her side, where he knelt and took her small hand in his.

"No, no," she said, hanging on to him tightly. "He went to see you last night and he didn't come home."

"Went to see me?" Matthew asked, frowning, utterly confused.

"Yes," she said, looking at him with tear-filled eyes. "To your party. They found out about it. I know they did."

"Who did?" Matthew asked, putting his arm around her to help her to stand.

"The family," she said, clinging to him. "Please you must help him. You must help my Noah."

Noah? Why did that seem familiar?

Could she mean Noel?

"I will," Matthew said. "I promise. Do you have any idea where he might be?"

"The last time this happened, they kept him in the stable," she said.

The last time this happened?

Oh, shit.

"Cal!" Matthew yelled over his shoulder. "A little help, please."

"What do you need?" Cal asked, bounding up the stairs.

"Can you take care of her?" Matthew said, transferring the woman gently into Cal's arms. "Make sure she's all right. I need to go find Noel."

Cal's eyebrows lifted. "You know where he is?"

Matthew was already halfway down the stairs. "I know where to look."

When he reached the second floor, he saw Dillon lying crumpled on the floor, dabbing at the blood trickling from his mouth.

"You can't do this!" Dillon cried, pushing up to balance on his forearm. "I'm calling the police."

"Go right ahead," Matthew said as he dashed down the final flight of stairs. Elaine was waiting for him at the bottom of them. Lucy stood behind her, arms wrapped around herself as if to try and hold everything together.

"What do you think you're doing?" Elaine said, her eyes a little wild, her color high. "You can't just barge in here and start going through my house like you own the place. I don't care how much money you have." She reached for him.

Matthew shook her off, evading her grasp. "Don't worry," he said. "I'm leaving." And true to his word, he pushed his way out the front door and darted down the steps.

Oh my God, he thought. Could it be true? Was it possible that Noel could be the old woman's grandson, Noah? Was he somewhere on the property, being held a prisoner or maybe even worse? What was going on, and how could it have happened under everyone's noses?

He sprinted across the yard, knowing the way well, even though he hadn't been there for years. He remembered that crazy night of the barbeque, stealing away with Charlie, and the first time he'd visited, when he'd ridden over on The Bean and met that kid with the great smile...

A smile with dimples.

Just like Noel had.

Actually, we did meet. Years ago. I was just a kid. So I'm sure you don't remember.

Maybe not then, but Matthew did now.

"Oh, God," he whispered as he ran, cursing himself for not putting the pieces together faster. "Oh my God!"

When he got to the stable, he yanked open the barn door. A man came out to greet him from what looked to be an office of some kind. He had a livid bruise high on his cheek and another larger, yet less vividly colored one on his throat.

"Can I help you?" the man asked, his tone anything but

friendly, his voice rough, as if he were a pack a day smoker.

"I'm looking for Noah," Matthew said, watching as the other man's face darkened when he heard the name.

"Don't think I know anyone named Noah," the man said, coming to stand toe-to-toe with Matthew, his hands clenched at his side.

"That's not what I heard," Matthew said, trying to push past him.

The man put his hand on Matthew's shoulder, intent on stopping him. "What do you think you're--?"

Matthew didn't even let him finish. He was done with waiting, with searching, with worrying. Noah was there. He knew it. And Matthew would be damned if he'd let this asshole stand in his way. He reached back and let his fist fly. It caught the man on chin. He made a sound of surprise, then dropped like a bag of rocks to land unmoving at Matthew's feet.

Matthew looked down at him, scowling, and shook out his hand. One punch and his knuckles had turned tender and sore. Yet all the same, he could feel a smile coming on.

Cal had been right all those years before—it was kind of fun to give an ass-kicking to a guy who had one coming.

Now where was Noah?

Matthew called his name. But he didn't get a response. If Noah's grandmother was right, though, and he was being held here, there weren't all that many places he could be. Matthew headed for the nearest closed door.

When he opened it, his heart dropped and shattered.

Oh, no.

Noah.

At first, Matthew feared he might be dead.

The man he'd been searching for lay slumped against the wall, curled over so that his knees were drawn up near his chest and his head hung heavy. Blood coated the side of his face, matting his hair and wetting the collar of his shirt. His hands and feet were tied, and he was gagged. His eyes were closed.

He wasn't moving. From where he stood, Matthew couldn't even tell if Noah was breathing.

"Noah?" Matthew said softly, falling to his knees at Noah's side, and reaching out to touch him. On his cheek, his shoulder, his chest. When that broad expanse lifted and fell beneath his palm, Matthew bowed his head and breathed a sigh of relief.

Oh, thank God.

Thank God.

He was alive.

"Noah? Hey... It's okay, man. It's all right. I'm here."

Working as quickly as he could, Matthew struggled to free Noah from the ropes that bound him. Only his fingers felt clumsy all of a sudden, strangely thick and stiff. It wasn't until he'd eased the gag from Noah's mouth, and laid him flat to rest on the floor that Matthew realized his own body was trembling.

"Just take it easy. Okay?" Matthew said, shrugging out of his jacket and draping it over the wounded man. It was chilly in the stable and Noah had apparently been out there all night. Matthew didn't know much more than basic first aid, but he was pretty damned sure hypothermia wasn't going to do Noah any favors.

Looking around, he spied an old woolen blanket folded on one of the tack room shelves. Pushing to his feet, he grabbed that and one of the saddle pads stored alongside it, before returning to Noah's side.

"Don't worry," he said, lifting Noah's head slightly to slide the pad underneath it. "I've got you. You're gonna to be all right. You're gonna be fine. You'll see." Shaking out the blanket, he tucked that around him as well.

Still, Noah didn't open his eyes, didn't move at all. Matthew began to wonder who he was saying the words for—Noah or himself.

"Hey, did you find him? Oh, my God."

Matthew started, then realized it was Cal's voice he heard. He looked over his shoulder and saw his friend framed in the doorway.

"Is that your boy?" Cal asked quietly.

"Yeah." Matthew nodded, then turned his attention back to Noah. He took hold of his hand. "They hurt him, Cal."

"I already called nine-one-one for the grandma," Cal said, coming to kneel beside Matthew. "They'll be here soon."

"Thanks," Matthew said. He felt young all of a sudden in a way he hadn't in years, like this was unknown territory and he was miles away from anything, without a compass or a map. "Can you do me a favor?"

"Name it."

Matthew met Cal's concerned gaze. "Would you mind calling my dad?" Part of Matthew felt embarrassed for wanting his family's support. Part of him didn't know how any of them were going to get through this without it."

"Sure," Cal said, reaching out and clapping Matthew on the shoulder. "I think having the old man around is probably a good idea."

"It's just..." Shaking his head, Matthew struggled to find the right words. "What the hell is going on here?"

"I don't know, Matt," Cal said, pressing to his feet. "But we'll get it sorted out. You stay with Noel. I'll keep an eye on everything at the house. When the paramedics arrive, I'll bring them out to you first."

"Thanks. I appreciate it. And Cal...?"

"Yeah?"

"His name is Noah."

As he watched Cal walk away, Matthew felt Noah's fingers twitch against his own.

"Noah?" he said, bending over him. Matthew took his free hand and rubbed his reddened knuckles gently against Noah's cheek. "Noah? Come on, man. Open your eyes. I want to make sure you're okay."

Matthew watched as Noah tried to do what had been asked of him. He frowned and moaned, his head turning slowly, restlessly against the floor before at last he was able to lift his lashes and look up.

"Matthew?"

"Yeah," Matthew said, giving his hand a squeeze. "I'm here."

"What are you...?" Noah whispered, his face pinched with what Matthew guessed might be effort or pain, his question left hanging, unfinished.

"You forgot your hat," Matthew told him, smiling, his thumb smoothing slowly over the back of Noah's hand.

"What?" Noah asked, his eyes swimming in their sockets, clearly not following.

"Nothing," Matthew said, leaning down to press a kiss to his forehead. "It's nothing. Just... try and stay awake for me. Okay? Help should be here soon."

"'kay," Noah whispered, fighting to keep his attention on Matthew, as if that somehow made it easier for him to stay aware.

Matthew understood the desire to maintain contact, and kept his gaze locked on Noah.

He had already lost him once. He wasn't going to let that happen a second time.

The first day or so after he'd been rescued, Noah found life confusing. He was only awake in fits and starts. His vision remained unclear and he sometimes couldn't remember conversations he'd supposedly had.

All perfectly normal given the concussion he'd suffered, his doctor told him.

That wasn't all she had to say.

"All in all, you were pretty lucky, Noah," Dr. Fallon said, her whiskey smooth contralto somehow making all the medical mumbo-jumbo that much easier to take. "I was most concerned about the blow you'd received to the head. But all the tests came back negative. There's no bleeding in the brain, and we were able to close up the wound without any problem. I want you to take it easy the next few days, and take Tylenol as necessary for the pain. I'll also need you back in about a week to get the stitches out. Otherwise, everything should heal up just fine."

"Good," he said, lying back against the pillows, his lashes

feeling heavier than they should. Dr. Fallon had told him he would probably feel tired for a while, that fatigue was natural given all he'd been through. Still, Noah couldn't help but feel badly about how much he was sleeping. He didn't think he'd ever been so lazy in his entire life.

"As for the rest of your injuries—your temperature is back to normal and we got you rehydrated without any trouble. I'm sure your bruises hurt like hell. But you're fortunate in that it's all soft tissue damage. No major organs were affected, no internal bleeding, no broken bones. Just take the Tylenol and try not to overdo it. If you can follow those instructions, I see no reason why you can't go home tomorrow morning."

"Home," he murmured, frowning, his thumb rubbing softly over the cotton blanket covering him. Noah wasn't even sure he understood what that word meant anymore.

"Hey, cheer up, kid," Dr. Fallon said. "That's good news."

Noah nodded, and did his best to smile. She was right. He had a lot to be happy about, to be thankful for. He knew that. He was going to recover and soon be good as new.

But most importantly, his grandmother was safe. That he did remember. She'd been in to visit him not long after he'd been settled in his room.

"Noah, sweetheart," she'd murmured from the wheelchair Matthew had used to transport her to Noah's side. She'd looked overjoyed, happier than Noah could ever recall having seen her, even while tears rolled down her pale cheeks. "You poor boy. You poor, dear boy."

"It's okay, Grandma. Don't cry. Everything is going to be all right now."

Matthew had assured Noah that it was, that his grandmother would be well looked after while Noah was in the hospital.

"I've got it covered, Noah," Matthew had said, his hip perched on the side of Noah's bed, his hand warm on Noah's arm. "All you need to worry about is getting better."

With the news that he was less than a day away from being discharged, Noah felt like he was holding up his end of the bargain. He just wasn't sure where he was supposed to go from there.

"Get some rest, Noah," his doctor said, patting him gently on the hip. "I'll check back with you before I finish my rounds."

"Thanks, Doctor," Noah said, watching her leave before closing his eyes and pressing his head back against the pillow. Maybe he would try and get some sleep before dinner. See if he couldn't get rid of some of this exhaustion.

"You too tired for some company?" asked a quiet yet familiar voice.

Any desire to sleep was instantly forgotten. Noah blinked open his eyes, and smiled. "Matthew. Come on in."

Grinning back at him, Matthew entered the room, dressed in a gray vee-necked sweater, jeans, and his leather jacket. He had a bag from the hospital gift shop in his hand.

"I brought you some more stuff to read," Matthew said, settling into the chair alongside Noah's bed and handing him the bag. "It's just a couple of news magazines and one of those sleazy gossip rags. If you don't feel like actually reading, you can look at the pictures in that last one, point and laugh. That's what I do."

"I haven't even finished the magazines you brought me yesterday," Noah protested, laughing with embarrassed pleasure at Matthew's generosity.

The man seemed to spend almost every minute of visiting hours, hanging out at Noah's bedside, and he never came without bringing Noah a present. So far, his gifts had included candy, a plant, balloons, an iPad loaded with music and games, magazines, a pair of sinfully soft flannel pajama pants, and some special kind of scented pillow Matthew's mom swore would help him sleep better. It was probably a good thing he was getting out of the hospital the following morning, Noah thought. If he stayed much longer, he had a feeling there soon wouldn't be space enough in the room for him.

"That's okay," Matthew said, smiling as he slipped out of his jacket and laid it over the back of his chair. "You can take them with you. I just ran into Dr. Fallon out in the hall, and she said she's letting you out of here tomorrow morning at ten."

"Yeah," Noah said, trying to pack as much enthusiasm as he could into the word. "She just told me."

"That's awesome," Matthew said. "I'll come by around nine-thirty and help you gather up all your things."

"You don't have to do that," Noah said.

Matthew shrugged. "What's an extra half hour if I'm going to drive you home?"

"About that..." Noah started, not sure how to ask what he needed to know. "Do you have any idea if Elaine is still there?"

"Where?" Matthew asked, seemingly confused.

"At the house," Noah said. "My house."

Matthew leaned forward in his seat, his hands clasped before him. "Noah, I'm taking you home with me. That's where your grandmother is. I thought that's where you'd want to be too."

Going home with Matthew? Staying with him at that luxurious palace known as Valley View, his grandmother safe and well, and staying with him. Who wouldn't want that?

But still...

"That's too much to ask," Noah said, shaking his head. "You've already done so much. I don't want to impose."

Sighing, Matthew pushed to his feet and came to sit on the bed beside Noah's hip. Reaching out, he took hold of Noah's hand. "First of all, you didn't ask. I offered. So don't be worried about imposing. Secondly, if you really want to go back to your place, I'll take you there. Because it seems to me too many people have told you what to do for far too long. But I have a feeling you might be lonely."

Noah frowned. "What do you mean?"

"Your stepmother and Dillon have been arrested and are being held without bail. Lucy is staying with some distant relative in Houston. Willis, your stable hand, is also behind bars. The only person setting foot on the property right now is the guy Cal's father has been sending over to take care of the horses. If you insist on going there, you'll have the place all to yourself."

"But that's..." Noah was having trouble taking it all in. "How did all that happen? What have they been arrested for?"

Matthew chuckled, his laughter utterly without humor. "Stealing your life and the life of your grandmother, and holding them hostage. More or less. You have to know what they did to you both was wrong, wrong in so many ways."

Noah nodded and looked away from Matthew. "I know that. I've known it for years. I just didn't think anyone would believe me if I told them."

"Yeah. Well, the one positive thing to come out of you being beaten bloody was it didn't exactly cast the rest of your family in the most positive light," Matthew said, giving his hand a squeeze. "From what I hear, Elaine had some story ready she was trying to spin, but the cops weren't buying it. They've been out at our place, talking to your grandmother, and apparently now they've got the feds involved too, as you were taken across state lines as a kid. I know they want to talk to you. But, with your head injury, Dr. Fallon convinced them to wait until you were discharged."

"Wow," Noah said, swallowing hard. He felt like he was dizzy even though he was sitting completely still. He wondered if the cause was his ever-present exhaustion, or simply a case of information overload. "S-so...what do I do now?"

"Now, you close your eyes and take that nap you were getting ready to take before I came in here and messed everything up," Matthew said, letting go of Noah's hand. Coming to his feet, he circled around the bed.

"Wait, you don't have to go," Noah said. He was tired, true. But he was always tired these days. He could sleep tonight when Matthew went home.

"I'm not going anywhere," Matthew assured him, returning to his seat in the chair and stretching out his legs on the bed next to Noah's. "I'm going to sit right here and read your magazines. And when dinner comes, I'm going to keep you company while you eat, then when you're not looking, steal your pudding."

Noah smiled, resting his head against the pillow and looked at Matthew through drooping lashes. "What makes you think I'll let you get away with that?"

"Because you're nice, Noah. Too nice for your own good. Now go to sleep. I promise not to take advantage of you."

Noah actually wouldn't mind if Matthew took advantage. At least not in certain ways. But aside from a chaste kiss or two, there had been no repeat of what they'd shared that night at the party. Of course, a hospital bed wasn't exactly conducive for romance. Still, he wished he knew where they stood.

Maybe he would ask Matthew.

Once he woke up from his nap.

When Matthew got to Noah's hospital room the following morning, Cal trailing along behind him for company and support, he found Noah sitting on the side of his bed, dressed in his new flannel pants and a white T-shirt. His hair was a mess, shaggy and finger-combed, the area above his ear shaved and marked by a row of neat black stitches. He had a purplish bruise on his chin and a cut across his eyebrow. He looked too thin, too worn, and the way he was sitting told Matthew his belly was still tender.

Matthew didn't think he had ever seen anything or anyone more beautiful in all his life. And he had come to take him home.

Lucky him.

"Your chariot awaits," Matthew said, leaning his shoulder against the door jamb.

Noah's face lit up. "There you are!"

"Hiya, kid," Cal said, peeking over Matthew's shoulder, and giving a little wave.

"Hey, Cal," Noah said. "I didn't expect to see you."

"Wanted to see how you were doing," Cal said, as both Matthew and he came into the room. "Last time I visited, you were kind of out of it."

Noah made a face. "Yeah. I have a feeling I'm going to be hearing a lot of that. I don't even really remember the first couple of days. I hope I didn't say anything embarrassing."

Matthew shrugged. "Other than confessing you hoped one day to receive a lap dance from William Shatner, and that you'd like nothing better than to live in a world made entirely of cheese—and really, aren't those two things sort of interconnected?—I'd say, no, you're good."

Noah arched a brow, a smile threatening on his lips. "Tell me I didn't."

"You didn't," Cal assured him. "Those are Matthew's dreams."

Matthew shot Cal an amused look, then tossed Noah the bag he was carrying. "Brought you something."

"You've got to cut that out," Noah said, shaking his head as he plucked the bag out of mid-air.

Matthew shrugged and sat beside him on the bed. "It's just

something for your trip home."

"Tell me it's shoes," Noah said, pulling on the bag's tie to open it. "Or at least slippers. I just now realized no one knows where mine are. I'm gonna be walking out of here barefoot."

"I think we've got that covered," Matthew said, trying not to feel smug.

Which was hard to do when he saw the stunned expression on Noah's face as he peered inside the bag. "Oh, my God. Matthew. What did you do?"

"I went to your house to pack up some clothes for you," Matthew said, refraining from mentioning how appalled he'd been to see the conditions under which Noah and his grandmother had lived. "Only it didn't seem to me like you had anything in your closet worth taking with you."

"Most of my things came from Dillon," Noah admitted as if embarrassed.

"That explains so much," Cal murmured.

"So I decided to get you something new to wear, something to celebrate your going home. You like?" Matthew asked, though he was already fairly certain of the answer.

"Yes. Of course I do," Noah said, smiling, his eyes shining in delight. "Thank you. You really shouldn't have."

"Why don't you go ahead and get dressed," Matthew said. "Cal and I will get started pulling together the rest of your stuff. Then we can get you out of here."

With a helping hand from Matthew, Noah eased to his feet and went into the bathroom to change. In the meantime, Cal got a box from the nurse's station that Matthew and he used to load up all of Noah's belongings. When Noah came back into the room, dressed in his new finery, they were ready to hit the road.

"Well," Cal said, giving Noah the once over. "Don't you clean up nice."

Matthew had to agree. He'd bought for Noah a buttery soft cashmere sweater in a deep wine color, a pair of professionally distressed denim jeans that fit him even better than his uniform pants had, black leather boots, and socks and underwear to go underneath.

"Looks like I did pretty well, guessing your size," Matthew said, smiling his approval. "You look good, Noah."

"Thanks to you," Noah said, running his hand along the sleeve of his sweater as if enjoying its velvety texture.

Matthew smiled. "Nah. I just worked with what was there. You made it easy."

It wasn't long before an orderly showed up with Noah's wheelchair. Cal offered to get the car and bring it around. Matthew stayed with Noah as they made their way to the hospital's exit, carrying the box of Noah's belongings and walking beside his chair.

"We came in my dad's Caddy," Matthew said, as they waited for Cal to pull up. "It looks like a hearse. But it's roomy and the ride is smoother than anything else he owns."

"I'm sure it's fine," Noah said, smiling up at Matthew from where he was seated, his dimples flashing. "It's not like I'm going to be picky."

"No," Matthew said, smiling back at him. "I know you're not."

Noah had some trouble getting into the car. But otherwise, the ride home was uneventful. When they pulled up outside Matthew's home, Matthew was surprised to see a beige, four-door sedan parked near the door.

"I wonder who that is," he murmured.

"Something that nondescript?" Cal said. "Sure looks like cops to me."

Matthew shook his head, his lips pressed flat in annoyance. "Couldn't they even let him come home and relax for a day before coming here to grill him?"

Noah laughed from the back seat. "I haven't done anything more tiring than sit since I got up this morning. If some police officer wants to ask me a few questions, I'm pretty sure I can handle it."

"Yeah well, if you change your mind, you let me know," Matthew said, getting out of the car and coming around to help Noah do the same. "We'll clear them out of here."

"Since when did you get so protective?" Noah asked, taking hold of Matthew's arm and using it as leverage to come to his feet.

Since I found you unconscious and covered in blood, Matthew wanted to say. Instead he smiled, his expression just a little bit forced. "I've been taking lessons from Cal."

"Learn from the best, son," Cal said, getting out of the car as well. "Learn from the best."

When they got inside the house, Matthew's father was waiting for them. "Noah, welcome to our home. I've got to tell you—you're looking better than the last time I saw you."

"Thank you, Sir," Noah said. Matthew's father had been one of those people who had visited Noah early in his convalescence. Judging by the look on Noah's face, Matthew would wager Noah couldn't recall much of what had been said between them. Matthew hadn't been there himself.

He wondered if there had been talk of cheese.

"I know your grandmother wants to see you, and you'd probably like to go upstairs and relax a bit, get a look at your room," Matthew's father said. "But before you do, there's an Agent McMillan here from the FBI. He's been waiting to talk to you. Do you think you feel up to it?"

Matthew looked over at him, worried. But Noah only shrugged. "Sure. Yeah, that would be fine."

Matthew's father gestured towards one of the rooms off the foyer. "He's in the library."

Noah headed in the direction Matthew's father had indicated; Matthew trailed after him. His father stopped him before he could follow Noah into the library.

"Son, I'm pretty sure the agent wants to see Noah alone."

Only just realizing what he'd done, Matthew felt his face heat with embarrassment. "Yeah. Yeah, of course."

"Come on, Matt," Cal said, wrapping his arm around Matthew's shoulder and drawing him away. "Something tells me you could use another cup of coffee."

Matthew nodded. "That sounds good. Noah, we'll be out here when you're done."

"Thanks," Noah said from the library doorway and went into the room.

Coffee sounded good, but staying with Noah sounded better, Matthew thought as Cal led him to the kitchen. He wondered why he was suddenly on his way to becoming a creepy stalker. And if the urge would be any easier to control now that he had Noah living with him, under the same roof.

The last time Noah had been at Matthew's house, he hadn't actually come into the library. He found it was a pleasant room with three walls covered floor to ceiling with shelves of books. The fourth contained a bank of windows that flooded the chamber with light. Comfy chairs were scattered about with footstools and reading lamps positioned appropriately. Near the center of the room was a long, heavy-looking table made of dark, polished wood. At it sat a man with thick salt and pepper hair and a neatly trimmed beard and moustache.

"Noah?" the man said, standing and offering his hand. "I'm Geoffrey McMillan, an agent with the FBI. I know you just got out of the hospital this morning, so I appreciate your agreeing to meet with me. I promise I won't keep you long. Why don't you sit down?"

"Thanks," Noah said, shaking the agent's hand, then taking a seat opposite him at the table. "I'm happy to help."

The agent pulled a small tape recorder from his jacket pocket. "I'll be recording our conversation," he said. "I'd like to ask you some questions, about your childhood and what it was like living with your stepmother and her family. Please know you're not in any trouble. I'm just trying to get a better picture of what went on at the house."

Noah nodded. "Okay, sure. Fire away."

With a small smile, Agent McMillan began asking his questions. Noah didn't find there to be any surprises. The agent wanted to know about their move, why Noah had never gone to school, what kind of work Elaine had expected of him, and how Noah had been disciplined when he'd made mistakes.

They spent a lot of time talking about what had happened the night of the fireworks and more recently when Noah had slipped away to go to Matthew's Halloween party. Agent McMillan was professional, yet sympathetic. Noah discovered he liked the man and his low, gruff voice.

"Noah, did your stepmother ever to talk to you about money?" McMillan asked after they'd been chatting nearly an hour.

"Money?" Noah echoed. "No, never. I never had any money of my own. Everything I had was given to me by Elaine."

"Did she ever say anything about how she was able to afford your home here in Texas?" McMillan asked. "Where the money came from for your stepbrother's education, the cars, the clothes, the horses? Did she ever tell you why, after marrying your father, she never took a job?"

Noah shrugged. "I assumed it was because she wanted to focus on being a mother."

McMillan looked at him for a moment, then leaned forward towards Noah, his hands folded on the library table. "Noah, one of the reasons I wanted to come here today, so soon after you were released from the hospital, was to share with you some information that has come to light in the midst of our investigation. This information is financial in nature and could have a significant impact on you and your life."

Noah's heart began to pick up speed. Something about the agent's solemn eyes and careful words was making him very nervous. "So tell me."

McMillan nodded, his lips quirking with a smile at Noah's impatience. "All right." He paused a moment to gather his thoughts. "When your father died, he'd only been married to your stepmother a matter of weeks. In all the excitement after the wedding, he hadn't had the chance to change the terms of his will. Are you aware of the way it was written?"

"No," Noah said. "I was barely five years old when my dad died. I have no idea about any of that."

"That's understandable," McMillan said, nodding. "The unfortunate thing is your stepmother used that to her advantage."

Noah frowned. "What do you mean?"

"Noah, you were your father's sole heir," McMillan said. "As you were a minor at the time of his death, it fell to Elaine to be the executor of the estate. Technically any money she spent should have gone to your care—housing, food, clothing, school."

Noah laughed, the sound short and sour. "That's not exactly the way things worked out."

"No," McMillan agreed. "I understand that. I'm telling you this now, though, so you realize whatever is left—the house, the land, the horses, anything in your stepmother's bank account— that's yours. She hasn't held a job since she married your father. She can't point to any other source of income than his estate."

Noah lifted his brows and slumped back in his chair, remembering all the times Elaine had taunted him by saying nothing belonged to him and everything belonged to her as his stepmother. "All that's mine?"

"Yes," McMillan said. "But there's one thing more."

Noah was almost afraid to hear it. Though the news had been nothing but good so far, it was wreaking havoc with his world view. "What is it?"

"You're eighteen now," McMillan said. "An adult. There was a risk for your stepmother in keeping you around. If you were ever to find out about the will, you could have challenged her in court, and you would have won."

"It never even occurred to me," Noah said softly.

"I know," McMillan said. "But that made me wonder why she'd maintained the status quo. So I did a little digging. With you being the only child of a single parent, your father had been very concerned about your wellbeing. Your grandmother and you were the only family he'd had left, and he'd wanted to make certain you were well provided for. So he took out a life insurance policy, one worth five million dollars."

Noah felt lightheaded, as if his brain had suddenly made a break for it out his ears. "Five...five million dollars?"

McMillan nodded. "Yes. It's payable to you when you turn twenty-one."

"How...how did Elaine think she'd be able to get her hands on that?" Noah wondered.

"This is all conjecture, of course," McMillan said. "But looking at what we know, it's fairly obvious your stepmother is an unscrupulous individual. Based on some of the decisions she made when you were younger, and the way she ignored the abuse you suffered while under her care, my guess is she would have been willing to use...extreme measures."

"Extreme?" Noah echoed in horror, even with everything he had been through growing up, he would never have believed Elaine capable of anything like that. "How extreme?"

McMillan shook his head. "She might have figured out a way to get you to sign over the money. If she accomplished that, it wouldn't have been all that difficult to make you disappear."

Noah was having trouble thinking at all anymore. "No one knew I existed except for Grandma."

"Exactly."

"Damn."

"Noah," McMillan said, reaching out to lay his hand on Noah's arm. "I know this is a lot to take in. But with everything that has happened to you, I wanted you to realize you have choices."

"What do you mean?"

McMillan shrugged. "You can sell the house or the horses, and use the money to go to school or travel. You could buy a place outside of Texas and build a new life for yourself entirely. In a few short years, you are going to be a very wealthy young man."

Noah rubbed his face with his hand. He was getting a headache. "I can't really believe any of this."

"I know," McMillan said. "And I'm sure, one or more of my colleagues will want to talk to you about it further. But you don't have to do anything right now. Just take some time, get yourself feeling better, and then think about what you want to do."

"Thanks," Noah said, giving him a small but sincere smile. "That's good advice."

"You're welcome. Now, if you'll walk me to the door, I'll get out of your hair."

Noah saw Agent McMillan out. When the door had closed

behind him, Noah stood there for a moment in the foyer, trying to decide what to do next.

Matthew's mother caught sight of him from the living room and came to stand opposite him. "Noah, honey. How are you feeling?"

He wasn't really sure. Still he said, "Good. I'm good, thanks."

"Your grandma just lay down to take a nap. Do you want something to eat?"

"No, thank you. I don't think I'm hungry. Have you seen Matthew?"

"I think he's upstairs," Matthew's mother said. "He said he wanted to make sure your room was ready. Why don't you come with me, and I'll show you where it is."

"Thanks," Noah said, following her up the stairs. "I also want to thank you for helping out my grandmother and me. You really didn't have to do that. But we so appreciate it. I don't know what we would have done otherwise."

"That's where you're wrong, hon. You and your grandma deserve every bit of help my family can give you," Matthew's mother said, looking over her shoulder at him as they climbed the steps. "I called your stepmother my friend for over ten years, and never once did I believe her to be anything other than a good person. I can't believe how wrong I was."

Noah smiled even though she couldn't see him. "Don't feel so bad. Elaine fooled a lot of people."

At the top of the stairs, Matthew's mother looked over at him and shook her head, her pretty mouth pulled down in a frown. "You're so sweet to say that. I just hope that woman gets everything that's coming to her and more."

Walking now, side by side, they traveled the length of a wide well-lit corridor until they came to a room whose door was ajar. Noah could hear music playing softly from inside. He thought it might be a song performed by Cal's band. Thanks to

Matthew's influence, he'd learned to enjoy their music.

"Here you go," Matthew's mother said. "I think we've got everything in there you'll need. But if we've forgotten anything, you be sure and let me know."

"I will," Noah told her. "But I'm sure it'll be great. Thanks again for everything."

"You're welcome, sweetie. I'll let you know when your grandma wakes up from her nap."

Smiling his farewell, Noah entered the room. Matthew was inside, sitting by the fire lit in the room's hearth, a book in his hand. When he saw Noah in the doorway, he looked up and grinned.

"Hey. Everything okay?" he asked.

"More or less," Noah said, and looked around.

The room was enormous. It wasn't even really a bedroom. It was more a suite, with a king-sized bed, two chaises, and assorted tables and chests on one side of the space, and two couches, a coffee table, end tables, and a wide screen television on the other side. A fireplace and archway separated what Noah could only imagine was supposed to be the sleeping area from the sitting area. Windows were abundant; the colors were warm and inviting. The far wall had a row of closet doors and an opening Noah suspected led to a bathroom. He had no doubt that room would prove to be as lavish as everything else.

Noah shook his head and closed his eyes, the day—his life—beginning to catch up with him. "This is...insane."

Matthew tossed aside his book and came to stand before him, reaching out to take Noah's arms in his hands and look into his face with concern. "Are you sure you're all right?"

Noah didn't even know how to answer that. But he opened his eyes. "Why wouldn't I be?"

Frowning, Matthew shrugged. "I don't know. You seem...freaked."

"Maybe I am," Noah admitted.

"Come here." Tugging softly, Matthew drew Noah into his arms. In all his life, Noah could only remember what it felt like to be held by his grandmother, her embrace tender but fragile, and nothing like this.

Matthew's arms were strong where they wrapped around him, and his face brushed Noah's with just a hint of whiskers, rubbing against his jaw like the softest sandpaper imaginable. Matthew smelled of spicy aftershave and some kind of herbal stuff he used to make his hair shiny and spiky. They hadn't done this the night of Matthew's party, hugging just to hug. But now, even though he knew he'd eventually want more, Noah found himself content.

Standing there, happy and safe, he realized the nagging doubts he'd had for as long as he'd known Matthew were finally silent, leaving nothing in their wake but peace. He wanted to tell Matthew about that, to explain why it was important. But before he could speak, Matthew did.

"Did that FBI guy say something to upset you?" Matthew asked quietly, his breath stirring Noah's hair.

Noah could feel Matthew's heart beating strong and sure against his chest. He found its gentle thump comforting. "Not like you'd think."

"What do you mean?"

Noah pulled away to meet Matthew's eyes. "Do you like me?"

Matthew managed to look both amused and annoyed. "What do you think?"

"Just tell me, please. I need to know."

Matthew's brow wrinkled. "Yes. Yes, of course I do."

"Why?"

Matthew looked at him a moment longer as if trying to figure out where Noah's questions were coming from. Noah wasn't even sure himself, so he wondered what conclusion Matthew might finally draw.

In the end, Matthew shook his head and lowered his eyes. "I don't know."

Noah supposed he should probably be concerned by Matthew's answer. But he didn't think the other man was being flippant, only honest. That, he could appreciate. "Why not?"

Matthew looked at him again, eased his arms away and took a step back. "What do you want me to say, Noah? That I think you're hot. That what you've overcome in your life terrifies me and makes me humble. That, even after everything you've been through, you're one of the kindest, most hopeful people I know. Do you want to know how happy I am when I'm with you? How when we're apart, I can't stop thinking about you. How when I see something funny or hear something interesting, my first thought is 'Wait till I tell Noah'. Is that what you want to hear?"

"Yeah," Noah said, feeling tears begin to well. He'd grown out of crying as a boy. It had never seemed to help and all his family had ever done was ridicule him for it. But now it appeared the urge was back, without him really understanding why. "Is that why you're so nice to me?"

Matthew must have seen his tears, and longed to ease them, because he smiled, small and gentle, as if inviting Noah to laugh instead. "Must be."

"Why you keep buying me things, and holding me when I'm sad or confused?" Noah said. "Why you were so patient with me when I didn't know anything about making love to you? Why you chose me out of a room full of people and then searched for me when you lost me, like you couldn't stand to let me go?"

"I guess so," Matthew said, holding his gaze.

"That sounds like love to me," Noah said.

"It might be," Matthew admitted. "I told my dad once: sometimes things just are. That's how it feels with you."

"Don't be afraid," Noah said, taking a step closer to him. "I've loved you from that very first day. When you rode up like some knight in shining armor on your big spotted horse, and were nice to me even though I smelled like horseshit."

"You don't even know me, Noah," Matthew said, as though it pained him to speak the words. "When you count it up, we've only been together a matter of days."

"I know you," Noah said, feeling more certain by the moment. "I know everything that matters, just like you know the same about me."

Matthew kept looking at him, as if he wanted to be convinced, but wasn't there quite yet.

"Do you know why I didn't say something to you that night?" Noah said, reaching out to take Matthew's hand. "Why I didn't tell you what my life was like and ask for your help?"

Matthew shook his head. "No."

"Because I was convinced you couldn't want me. Not like I wanted you."

"You didn't trust me?"

"No," Noah said, rubbing his thumb over the back of Matthew's hand. "It wasn't you. It was me. I was too scared. I didn't want you to feel like you needed to rescue me."

"I would have," Matthew said. "I would have done whatever it took to get you and your grandmother out of there."

"You did," Noah reminded him. "Even though I didn't want you to. And I will always be grateful."

"Why are you telling me this now?" Matthew asked, reaching down to capture Noah's other hand. "What's changed?"

Noah smiled, one of the bright, wide ones he knew Matthew loved. "As it turns out, I don't need rescuing anymore."

Matthew smiled back at him, though it appeared he wasn't entirely sure why. "What do you mean?"

Keeping hold of Matthew's hands, Noah told him of the

conversation he'd had with Agent McMillan. When he was finished, Matthew pulled him close once more, hugging him hard, more in celebration this time than in comfort.

"Man, that's great news," Matthew said, his face buried against Noah's neck. "Great news. I'm so happy for you."

Noah chuckled, pulling back to look Matthew in the eye. "I'll admit—the more I think about it, I'm happy too."

"Look at you," Matthew said, beaming now, so pleased for Noah it was as if his good fortune were Matthew's own. "I was so worried about you. But it's like you got your very own fairy tale ending. Good wins out and evil is banished. Here I was, all set to look out for you. Only it turns out you don't need me at all."

Noah shook his head and took hold of Matthew's arms. "That's where you're wrong."

Matthew frowned. "Why?"

Noah did his best to appear serious. "I want a happy ending."

Matthew lifted his brows. "Sounds to me as if you got one."

"Mostly," Noah said, nodding. "I just need one last thing."

"What's that?" Matthew asked.

"My Prince Charming," Noah said, the corners of his lips beginning to lift. "Every good fairy tale has one."

Matthew was starting to smile now as well. "Got anyone in mind?"

"I kinda do," Noah said. "You think you're up for the job?"

"What would I have to do?" Matthew asked.

"You could start by kissing me," Noah said.

"I can do that," Matthew said.

And he did.

~*~*~*~

And they all lived happily ever after.